WISHES, SINS, AND THE WISSAHICKON CREEK

A SHORT STORY COLLECTION

PJ DEVLIN

Pati

12/11/22

To Liz,
    a new friend,
    PJ Devlin

Benezet Street Press

Benezet Street Press

AUTHOR'S NOTE

Dedicated to my brother, David, who left us his light.

I've known I was a writer from the moment I learned the alphabet and put pencil to paper. I wrote stories throughout grade school, high school, and college. I love entering *the fictive dream* where a story takes me beyond my original concept, and characters enter uninvited, fully formed and demanding voice. Stories become reckonings where wonder, folly, love, hate, sadness, joy, rage, and regret seep from the subconscious to forge paths to understanding, sometimes epiphany.

Readers often ask: Is your story autobiographical? The answer is, No. My characters aren't versions of me. Rather, I become the characters. Although my characters live and breathe through me, each is a being apart just as children are beings apart from their parents. Fictional characters, like children, say and do the unexpected, living on the page on their own terms. That's the dream. That's the wonder.

Setting is the element which emanates from my personal history. In order for characters to make their ways through complicated situations, I drop them in places I know well – most often, they find themselves near the Wissahickon Creek which flows from Montgomery County, PA through northwest Philadelphia until gushing into the Schuylkill River.

It's hard to describe the draw of the Wissahickon Creek, yet each person I've met who's hiked, biked, or ridden horses over fifty miles of rocky trails surrounded by woods feels a sense of ownership and enchantment. In the Preface to the wonderful four volume book, *Metropolitan Paradise: The Struggle for Nature in the City, Philadelphia's Wissahickon Valley 1620 - 2020*, authors David Contosta and Carol Franklin write — "Both of us have a dogged and perverse devotion to Philadelphia, and like so many Philadelphians, we are hopelessly in love with Wissahickon Park . . ."

My dreams of childhood ebb and flow like the branch of the creek which ran through once-farmland behind our home. Neighborhood kids spent summers at the creek skipping stones, floating twigs, and hopping from rock to rock. In winter, we dragged sleds up a hill to race down to the edge of or into the creek for a frigid walk home.

Time and again, we walked down Wissahickon Avenue past the Morris Arboretum and Chestnut Hill College to enter Forbidden Drive, the graveled towpath along the Wissahickon Creek. Dense trees blocked all but shimmers of sunlight. Rough rocky ridges beckoned us to the narrow trails above both sides of the creek. As we clambered over boulders and through patches of poison ivy, we imagined we were Indian children searching for chestnuts to grind into meal. A favorite destination was across the red covered bridge and up a rocky path to the giant marble statue of Indian Chief Tedyuscung perched on a promontory, shielding his eyes as he searches westward.

While not every story in this collection is set along the Wissahickon, each story has a Philadelphia heart. Some are long, some are short, some are set in the present, some in the past.

PJ Devlin

1

I WISH IT EVERY DAY

This warm December morning, Pastorius Park in Germantown is deserted. I lock my car and approach the monument to Francis Daniel Pastorius.

A huge marble statue of a bare-chested woman, *Civilization*, rests on a granite base. In her right hand, she bears a light guiding the way to the future. I sense Pastorius would consider the statue as I do — a tombstone incompatible with his love of living things.

Research on Pastorius for my blog on gardening — *Growing Old* — has brought me to my hometown. For forty years, I've shunned Philadelphia, returning only for births, graduations, weddings, and funerals — my parents' funerals. Now that our son and daughter are grown, my husband, Dominic, wants to come home. He longs to comfort his mother in her waning years and spend weekends with his brothers drinking beer and watching the Eagles. He studies Zillow for listings in the neighborhoods where we grew up. Before I left our home in Maryland, Dominic said, "Drive around. Think about it."

Instead, I think about a bitter cold December day in 1975.

Before I drive to the central library downtown, I stop at a coffee shop in Chestnut Hill. While I sip my drink, I study the regional rail schedule. The local train runs the same route my great-grandfather rode until October 1918, when he joined 16,000 Philadelphians who succumbed to the Spanish flu.

"Mary Edwards?"

A white-haired woman approaches my table, a steaming cardboard cup in her hand. Behind tortoise-shell glasses, her cloudy blue eyes consider me in a familiar way. White Linen's sweet scent lingers before I realize who she is.

"Julia," I say, "it's been a long time."

I wonder if it's been long enough.

JULIA DUPONT and I made unlikely high school friends, a relationship brought about by the alphabetical order of our last names. She had elegant manners and refined diction, and wore clothes that fit her slender build perfectly. Her long blonde hair, blue eyes, and quiet laughter attracted football players and awkward boys with cracking voices — and me.

I entered high school a shy pudgy girl with freckles. I spoke row-house Philly and wore clothes from the Bargain Basement. No girl in my neighborhood — not even older girls whose gum cracking and throaty laughs I copied — fascinated me like Julia. She was the light guiding my way to a future I never imagined existed.

The first day of freshman year, I inched down the hall along the lockers, hunched against jostles and jolts from hooting boys and hip-swinging girls. As soon as I found my homeroom, I collapsed in my assigned seat. After I checked my book bag for pencils and notebooks, I glanced into the wide blue eyes of the girl in the desk beside me.

"I'm Julia DuPont," she said. "It's the first time my parents let me go to public school. Do you have any advice?"

This girl, so much cooler than me, asked me for advice?

"Don't wear high heels," I said, my only thought.

"You're so funny. Show me your schedule," she said.

After Julia compared our schedules, she said, "We have Algebra and English together, but I have Music when you have gym. Then we're together in Biology. I have gym last period when you have Spanish. But we both have fourth lunch."

The homeroom teacher entered then. All anxious chatter ceased when he slapped the desk with his ruler. From Julia's desk, a light flowery smell floated, an aroma I learned was *White Linen* cologne. The bustle of books left me disoriented, but after the teacher dismissed us, Julia waited while I slung my book bag over my shoulder. Together we found our way to Algebra and slid into desks next to each other.

Afterwards, as we parted ways in the hall, Julia called, "Meet you for lunch. Save me a seat."

BECAUSE OF JULIA, I was accepted. I was cool. Through her, I envisioned access to a world beyond a blue-collar job.

Throughout Freshman year I watched, listened, and learned. By April, I'd grown two inches and lost twelve pounds. I learned to iron my frizzy red hair and sort through clothes at Bargain Basement until I found hip-hugger jeans and Poor Boy sweaters with rips my mother mended. The day I wore a Mexican peasant blouse like Julia's, she noticed an uneven seam and puckered repair.

"Mary, you need to return that blouse. It looks like a second," she said, upper lip curled.

Despite burning cheeks, I managed to match her sneer.

"My aunt gave it to me, so Mom said I had to wear it."

At home I tossed the gauzy cream blouse with embroidered flowers and floppy sleeves into the back of my closet and left it there.

That summer I got a job at Bruno's Garden Center on the local bus line. Julia flew to her family's summer home in Switzerland to study at the Geneva Music Conservatory. While Julia's fingers swept polished ivory, mine dug through potting soil.

BY SENIOR YEAR, the two things I cherished were Julia's friendship and my job at the Garden Center.

In November, Julia spread college catalogs across a library table and divided them into colleges of music and colleges with botany majors. I leaned on my elbows watching Julia sort through them, head tipped, tongue poking between her teeth. She patted four catalogs, flung back her hair, and slid three other catalogs to me.

"I'm applying to Juilliard, Curtis, Manhattan, and Peabody," she said. "You should apply to Columbia, University of Pennsylvania, and Johns Hopkins. They're in the same cities as my schools. After we get accepted, we'll decide where to go so we stay close."

"We'll always be close," I whispered, wishing away doubt.

I hadn't told Julia, but I wouldn't go to college. The upper-class diction I emulated and the counterfeit designer clothes I wore disguised a blue-collar girl whose reach, I realized, exceeded her grasp. The day I'd gotten up the nerve to talk to my parents about college, my mother pressed her lips together while my father said, 'Mary, we're counting on you to help out.' I knew they relied on the $25 I gave them each week from my Garden Center salary. My little sister and brother always needed shoes, or coats, or cough medicine. My father worked at the Ironworks factory, but was laid off whenever orders slowed. My mother took in sewing but brought in few extra bucks.

I didn't consider us poor — we had food on the table and heat in winter — but my future earnings meant a better family car, a new refrigerator, a step away from constant worry. I was resigned to supporting my family, but resisted the thought of losing Julia, and the vision of a life of fine clothes, nice cars, international travel, and privilege. Deep inside, I suspected our flower of friendship might wither and die. I vowed to nurture it as long as possible.

After classes that November day, I met Julia at her locker. She greeted me with a warm smile and asked, "Garden Center today?"

After I nodded, Julia sighed. "The chorus director says I have to accompany some sophomore for the Winter Concert. I hope she can carry a tune. I have to stay late to practice. We'll catch up later."

THAT DAY, I reached the bus stop as the rusty green behemoth pulled away. I chased it, waving and yelling, until the driver screeched to a halt. I climbed the steps, croaked a thanks, and slid a quarter through the slot. I lurched down the aisle to a seat near the back doors. Black clouds billowed behind the sluggish bus. I leaned my head on the dingy window and gave in to the miserable thought I could no longer ignore: Soon Julia would realize I wasn't going to college.

Years before, when I told her I got a job at the Garden Center, she wrinkled her nose and asked why I'd work in such a dirty place. I claimed working at the Garden Center was equivalent to practicing piano — necessary preparation for my newly fabricated plan to become a botanist. To give credence to my lie, I studied hard and excelled in biology and chemistry. Weirdly, my bogus story became true. I loved working with flowers, shrubs, trees, vegetables, and fruit. I loved the smell and feel of dirt. I planted crocuses across the front of our house and thrilled each March when they blossomed. I wrote a paper on Edith Wharton and impressed Julia with my discovery of Wharton's passion for gardening along with her upper-class family background. 'You're just like Edith Wharton,' Julia liked to tease when I talked about the Garden Center.

As soon as the Bruno's Garden Center billboard came into view, I pulled the cord and heard the satisfying ding. The bus groaned to a stop, the doors folded open, and I hopped out. Before I crunched across the gravel parking lot, I gazed at the rakes, shovels, and stacks of fireplace logs displayed across the front. The earthy, smelly world inside those doors welcomed me, but Julia's elegant pristine world enchanted me.

I walked to the back and pushed through thick plastic strips to enter through the storage area. Fertilizer and weed killer smells blended with the organic odor of mulch. I envisioned my elderly self strapped to a hospital bed with tubes up my nose and a bag dripping fluid in my veins while a green-masked doctor frowned at my medical chart and muttered, 'She worked at the Garden Center.'

After I punched in, I slipped on my Bruno's Garden Center apron and found Bruno, a swarthy man, in his office.

"Hey, Freckles, we got lots ta do today," he said. "First, check last night's delivery and add it to inventory. Den make a nice display of da Christmas wreaths."

"Ya gotta gimme da clipboard if I'm gonna do dat," I told him.

The minute I walked through those plastic strips, the cultured diction I adopted around Julia gave way to my native tongue. I spoke like my neighborhood, like the guys who sold bags of soft pretzels on street corners, like the water ice ladies who appeared with their carts every summer.

I took the clipboard and scanned the orders. Before I turned away, Bruno cleared his throat.

"We gotta new guy startin' today — my nephew, Dominic. Show him da ropes, huh?" Bruno's deep brown eyes, beautiful in his rough pocked face, studied me. "He's a good one, Freckles, been through a lot. Treat him good, ya know what I mean?"

"Sure, no problem," I said. "He here yet?"

A woman whose squirming toddler smelled like overripe bananas pushed her cart toward the cash register. Bruno wiped his hands on his apron and squeezed into the check-stand to ring her up — two bunches of cut flowers and bricks of floral foam.

"We just moved into a house with a yard, and I want to plant some bulbs," she said. "What do you recommend for someone with a black thumb?"

"Freckles, what bulbs ya think dis nice lady'd like?"

"Dutch crocuses. They're pretty, they come up every March, and they're inexpensive, but you need to get them in the ground before it freezes. I'll get you a couple packs," I said, pleased Bruno asked me, and confident in my response.

After I placed four net bags — each with 20 bulbs — on the conveyer, the woman raised her eyebrows and asked, "Four?"

I smiled and nodded. "They're 75 cents each. You don't have to buy four, but I brought that many to help you remember how to plant them — four inches deep and four inches apart. Just be sure you plant them pointy end up."

The woman examined one of the bags, and smiled at her little boy. "Mommy will plant these when you take a nap. Don't tell Daddy, though. It'll be our surprise."

"Don't let da boy eat da bulbs," Bruno said. "Ya don't want kids or pets eatin' da bulbs."

As I carried the woman's bags to her car, I told her, "I love crocuses. They're the flower of happiness and rebirth."

Back inside, Bruno waited with crossed arms. "Ya know your flowers, Freckles."

A grey station wagon with fake wood-grain sides crackled across the parking lot. A young guy climbed out, held a hand over his eyes, and scanned the road before he slammed the car door shut and entered the Garden Center.

"Dominic!" Bruno wrapped his arms around the guy, who gave me a crooked smile over Bruno's shoulder.

Julia would have described Dominic as tough-looking. He wore tight black jeans and black T-shirt. A scar cut through his right eyebrow, and dark hair curled down the back of his neck. He wasn't much taller than me. With a broad nose and square jaw, one wouldn't call him handsome, but his blue eyes were striking in his olive complexion.

"Freckles, dis is my nephew. Where we gonna start him?"

"He can help check the delivery, am I right? Then we'll set out the wreaths." I glanced at the clock — ten past four. My bus passed the Garden Center at 7:38 p.m. Three hours to "show the ropes" to Dominic.

"Freckle's a smart girl, Dominic. She'll keep ya straight."

With Dominic following, I turned to see Bruno watching. I gave him a wave and thought how much I liked Bruno and this job.

In the storage area, Dominic heaved boxes onto flat utility carts and called out the items for me to check off.

"Where you from, Dominic?" I asked.

He set down a stack of fireplace logs and adjusted his work gloves.

"Whaddya need to know?"

"Where you live, where you go to school. You got brothers or sisters? Just asking." I tried to sound nonchalant.

Dominic returned to work while he talked. I learned he lived with his mother and three younger sisters in Mount Airy and was a senior at Germantown High School. Two years ago, Dominic's father, a city cop, died in the line of duty after he saved a three-year-old boy from a speeding truck. The truck clipped his dad, who stumbled and smacked his head on the curb.

"The weird thing is, Dad came home around 9:30 that night after he checked himself out of the emergency room. He was like that, you know? Never wanting any fuss. He told Mom it was just a bruise and a bump, nothing to worry about. After midnight, Mom heard him gurgling. She tried to get him to wake up, but that was it. He left us."

"I'm sorry," I said, and fought back tears.

My father's hands and arms were crisscrossed with burns from the Ironworks. One night I heard him tell Mom a guy's arm got mangled in the machinery, but Dominic was the first person I knew who lost a parent. He hoisted the last box on the cart and leaned against the shelves.

"Yeah, it's tough on my mom and sisters. I do what I can. It got easier after I got my driver's license. We get survivors benefits, and the FOP — Fraternal Order of Police — helps out some, but Mom needs help with the girls, the house, money, everything." He steered the loaded cart at me. "Hop on. I'll give you a ride to the front."

I tucked the clipboard under my arm and climbed on a long flat box filled with grapevine wreaths for Christmas crafters. The cart jerked. I lurched backward, but Dominic steadied me. His muscles were taut as he pushed the heavy cart, and a jolt like electricity coursed through me. The twisty ride ended when a booming voice echoed down the aisle.

"Whadda youse guys think yer doin'? For da love a Mike, get down from dere, Freckles, before ya fall and break yer neck."

Dominic helped me down. Our eyes met. I bit my lip to keep from laughing. Bruno, brow furrowed, shook his head. But before he moved away, I caught his smile.

After my shift, in a casual voice I asked Bruno, "When you need me to show your nephew more ropes?"

"He works Tuesday, Thursday, Saturday, Sunday," Bruno said. "Dat good for you?"

THAT NIGHT while Mom put my sister and brother to bed, and Dad watched TV, I called Julia from the kitchen phone. The smell of cold grease rose from the garbage can.

"Bruno's nephew, Dominic, started at the Garden Center today," I said, my voice cheery in anticipation of a rush of questions. "He's a really nice guy."

Julia yawned. "That sophomore girl's a good singer. Her name's Connie. Mary, can we talk tomorrow? I have to finish my homework."

"Sure," I said, swallowing disappointment.

I felt like I'd been scolded. Don't be an ass, I told myself. Julia's busy. Tell her about Dominic tomorrow.

THE NEXT MORNING, Julia missed our classes, and I worried she was sick, but before lunch, as I shoved my books in my locker, she appeared beside me.

"Mary! I want you to meet Connie. She has perfect pitch."

Although our eyes didn't meet, the sallow-faced girl hovering behind Julia offered an awkward smile. Julia's pleased expression reminded me of my mother's when she put a plate of cookies on the table.

"Hi." I turned to Julia. "Wait 'til I tell you about Dominic."

"Connie and I need to practice, but we'll talk Friday when we go to the mall."

Before they hurried away, Julia squeezed my hand.

AFTER SCHOOL FRIDAY, I waited by Julia's yellow Camaro, eager for our weekly trip to the mall and movies. I pulled the collar of my pea coat tight and wished I'd worn gloves. At the sound of Julia's brisk footsteps, my heart raced. I couldn't wait to tell her about Dominic.

"Hi, Mary," Connie's voice, unfamiliar although pleasant, sent a shudder through me.

What the hell, I thought. I narrowed my eyes.

"What's wrong, Mary?" Julia asked, voice rich with concern.

"You giving Connie a ride home?"

"I invited her to the movies with us," Julia said.

"Julia says you and I have lots in common so we should get to know each other," Connie said.

I turned away from her crooked-toothed smile to hide my disgust. Connie and I had nothing in common.

Julia unlocked the passenger-side door. I waited for Connie to slide in the back, but she stepped aside. I didn't move.

Julia raised her right eyebrow. "Hop in, Mary. Connie's bigger than you. She'll be more comfortable in front."

DESPITE MY IRRITATION, I was looking forward to seeing *One Flew Over the Cuckoo's Nest.*

As we approached the ticket counter, Connie clapped. *"The Adventures of the Wilderness Family!* This is so great, Julia. I never go to the movies. Oh, I forgot to bring money. Can you pay for my ticket?"

"We're seeing *One Flew Over . . ."*

Julia nudged me. "Next time."

In the theater, Connie, chomping buttered popcorn and slurping a 7-Up, sat between Julia and me. When the movie ended, I had no appetite for the pizza Julia and I always got. I had no appetite for anything.

"Bruno wants me in early tomorrow," I said. "The Garden Center gets busy for Christmas."

Connie stared. "You work at the Garden Center?"

I shrugged and checked my watch. "There's a bus in ten minutes. I better get home."

Julia stiffened. Her warm blue eyes turned steely grey. My stomach knotted. As I hurried away, my knees wobbled. I'd never seen Julia so angry. She's really pissed, I told myself. You did it now.

Just before I entered the revolving doors to go out, heavy footsteps pounded behind me.

"Mary, wait," Connie called. "Julia says since we live near each other, I should ride the bus home with you."

My face tightened as if a gun were jammed in my back. I pretended I didn't hear, and hurried to the bus stop, praying to board before Connie caught up. But when the bus lurched to a stop, she arrived, panting. She climbed in ahead of me and told the driver I was paying for both of us. My hands knotted in fists, but I dug two quarters out of my change purse and paid the fares.

The bus was full. Shoppers with vacant expressions filled almost every seat. Five rows back, Connie squeezed in next to a red-faced woman who stared out the window. I clutched an overhead strap and stood wide-legged in the aisle near Connie. The mothball scent from her worn red coat made me sneeze. I focused on the dark window until she tugged my sleeve. I bristled like a cat.

"That was fun. I don't go out much. I work, too, like you."

"Oh?"

My brusque tone didn't keep Connie from launching into an exhaustive personal history. She and her mother lived in rooms at the Peaceful Days Nursing Home run by the Episcopalians, where her mother cleaned and cooked. Connie didn't know where her father was — he left ten years ago. Her older brother, John, joined the army and was stationed in Texas.

Every day, as soon as she got home from school, she helped served dinner to the old folks. Weekends, she wheeled them to the recreation room, where they loved to sing with her. Sundays, she sang with the church choir. Now the old ladies were all upset because she's been staying late at school to practice for the Winter Concert.

"Singing with Julia playing piano is so great," Connie said, wide-eyed. "You and Julia should visit Peaceful Days. Julia could play piano, and we could sing Christmas songs for the old folks. They'd love that!"

"I don't sing," I said.

The bus approached Peaceful Days, and Connie reached over her seat-mate to pull the cord. As the bus whined to a stop, she pressed against me.

Just before the doors folded open, she said, "You and Julia are my best friends."

Two stops later, I stomped off the bus and inhaled the diesel-filled air. Best friends? Connie's words burned like acid.

Saturday, Bruno met me at the door.

"Dere you are, Freckles. Da insecticide order came in last night. Dominic moved it to da floor."

Bruno returned to his ancient wood-grain radio and turned the dial until Elvis Presley's bluesy voice emerged — *Decorations of red . . .* He flipped on the PA system, and the Garden Center filled with tinny Christmas music.

Before I unloaded the boxes of insecticide, I turned over a bucket to sit on. While I arranged gallon jugs by brand and color — green, black, red, blue, and white — I tried to avoid inhaling the sweet scent of insect death. Outside, a red Santa hat bobbed between stacks of Christmas trees. Dominic, I thought, and smiled.

After I finished with the insecticide, I stomped on the empty cardboard boxes and piled them up. The scratchy piped-in Christmas music suddenly transformed into a breathtaking song — *And folks dressed up like Eskimos . . .*

I turned toward the sound, and my heart dropped. Connie's singing brought customers to a standstill. When the song ended, an elderly couple clapped. Now I understood Julia's appreciation for Connie's voice, but not for Connie. I started to drag the empty boxes to the storage room, but she caught me. Her cheeks shone red. A woman with patchy skin and yellow-grey hair stood behind her.

"Mary, this is my mom, Madge Foley. When I told her about you, she said we could drive to the Garden Center so she could meet you."

Ambushed. "Hi," I said.

Mrs. Foley reeked of cigarettes and mothballs. She stared at me with an expression so hopeful I felt uncomfortable.

"Were you looking for something specific?" My eyes flitted across the store seeking salvation.

"We might take a look at the Christmas trees," Mrs. Foley said.

"Nice singing," I told Connie, who stared at the insecticide jugs, then spoke to her mother. "Nice to meet you, Mrs. Foley, but I have to get back to work."

"Won't you help us get a Christmas tree?" Connie asked, reproachful.

"I don't do trees. The guy outside takes care of them," I answered.

I dragged the crushed boxes to the back of the store, feeling violated. My right eye twitched. In the storage room, I circled pallets of mulch, praying for Connie and her mother to leave. My face flushed, my mind raged. I wanted to dump a bag of mulch on Connie's head. Was I supposed to befriend Connie because Julia did? After I figured enough time went by, I headed to the front.

At the cash register, Bruno smiled his scary smile at two elderly customers and handed them the receipt. "Tanks fer yer bizness. Let me help ya to da car." He turned to me. "Where ya been hidin', Freckles? Work da cash register, will ya?"

Not a minute after I slid behind the register, Dominic appeared. A blush rose to my cheeks at his smile.

"How ya doing, Mary?" He handed me a Christmas tree price ticket with $15 slashed through, and $7.50 scribbled over it. He shrugged. "I marked it down for your friends. I'm going outside to tie it on their car. Ya wanna take lunch break together?"

They're not my friends, was on the tip of my tongue when I noticed Connie and her mother moving toward the register. "Sure, sounds good," I said.

Connie thumped a gallon of Annihilator Insecticide on the conveyor belt, and her mother added a bag of plastic snowflakes. I stepped on the floor switch, and the bug killer rolled down the belt.

"$7.50 for the tree — the guy's tying it on your car — $6.50 for the Annihilator, and 99 cents for the snowflakes. With tax, that's $15.75."

Connie's mother fumbled in her purse, digging deep. Then she checked each of her pockets. She spread crumpled dollar bills on the belt and a handful of change.

"If you take off the tree and snowflakes, will $7.87 cover the insecticide?" Mrs. Foley asked, eyes red-rimmed and weary. "Connie says we need the Annihilator for roaches."

Connie's hungry eyes met mine. I looked away.

"This once I'll give you my discount. That will be $7.87 exactly."

Mrs. Foley smiled. "You're right, Connie. Mary's a very nice girl."

"See you later, Mary," Connie said.

She handed the snowflakes to her mother, and headed for the door, hugging the Annihilator jug.

Mrs. Foley lingered, her eyes on mine. "It's so nice Connie finally has friends her own age."

As soon as Mrs. Foley was outside, Bruno walked over.

"No discounts fer friends, Freckles. Ya know da policy."

"They aren't my friends," I told him. "I felt bad the lady didn't have enough money. Take eight bucks out of my pay."

Dominic joined us and moved beside me. "I cut the price on the tree. Take eight bucks outta my pay, too." He knit his brows. "God, Mary, where'd you get friends like them?"

"They're not my friends," I said.

Dominic studied me, a confused expression on his face.

"Youse guys are a piece a work." Bruno shook his head. "Birds of a feather. I catch either of ya givin' away my stock again, I'll can ya both."

At our lunch break, Dominic bought two Cokes from the machine. I gave him half my baloney sandwich.

"We oughtta grab some slices after work some time," Dominic said. "Whaddya think?"

"As long as it's near a bus route so I can get home."

"Don't worry about that. I got the car. So what's the story with the singer and her Mom?"

I made a ball with our trash and tossed it into the trash container. After I swigged the last sip of Coke, I shook my head and shrugged.

"I have no idea. My best friend, Julia, has to play piano when the girl — Connie — sings at the Winter Concert. Julia must feel sorry for her because she invited her to the movies with us. But Connie's not my friend. I don't really like her." I was relieved to say those words out loud.

"We better get back before Bruno throws a fit." Dominic pushed aside the plastic strips. "Just tell the girl, Don't take it personal, but I plan to spend all my free time with my new friend, Dominic."

As he swaggered away, his words looped through my mind, and I smiled.

SUNDAY NIGHT, the phone rang. My mother called up the stairs, "Mary, Julia's on the phone."

Julia? My heart leapt then clenched. I was desperate to talk, but felt shy and uncertain. I feared this conversation.

"Mary, why didn't you call?" Julia asked in her warmest voice.

I swallowed, hoping to sound normal. "I figured you'd be hanging out with Connie."

"God, Mary, after the Winter Concert, I'm done with her." Julia's tone was conspiratorial.

"I thought you liked her."

"Please. She's not like us." Julia paused then said, "She's common. I tried to be nice, but she follows me everywhere. She thinks we're friends. I can't shake her off."

"*Macrobdella decora,*" I said.

"What?"

"*Macrobdella decora* — the North American leech." My voice filled with glee.

"You're so funny, Mary." Julia's laughter rang sweet. "You're coming to the concert, right? I need you to help me escape."

"I work Thursdays," I told her.

"I need you, Mary. We'll go to HoJo's after the concert."

A smile spread across my face. Julia needs me. We're okay.

"I'll see if I can get off."

"Good. Now tell me about this boy," Julia said.

"His name's Dominic DeMarco. He's really nice, Julia. I like him. I'm pretty sure he likes me, too." I hadn't told my parents or anyone else about Dominic. I felt happy talking about him now.

"Didn't you tell me he's Bruno's nephew?" Julia asked. "Where's he from?"

"The city. His dad was a Philly cop who died two years ago."

"Sad. Cops don't make much money, do they?"

I imagined Julia twirling her hair.

"Dominic said it's been tough since his dad died. He helps his mom with his three little sisters."

I heard Julia breathing, but she didn't say anything.

"Julia, you there?"

She let out her breath. "I'm only saying this because we're friends. Be careful, Mary. You don't want to get involved with someone who'll bring you down."

"What?" I stuttered. "Dominic's great. I like him. What are you saying?"

"Don't get upset. Just . . . I hate to see you slumming."

"Dominic isn't slumming," I whispered.

Julia's lovely laughter floated through the phone. "It's a joke, Mary. I'm sure he's a nice guy."

"Just a joke," I said.

"Make sure you get off Thursday for the concert," she said. "You're my lifesaver."

After I hung up, I climbed the stairs, lay on my bed, shut my eyes, and ached from the bruises on my heart. But Julia needed me.

When I asked to work Friday instead of Thursday, Bruno said, "Sure, no problem."

ALL WEEK the weather was crappy — cold, fog, drizzle, snow flurries, and hail. Thursday, the principal announced the Winter Concert would start at 6:00 instead of 8:00 because of expected snow. Instead of walking home after school then back in the cold, I helped set up chairs in the auditorium and placed programs on every seat. From backstage, Connie's voice rang out loud and pure. Like her or lump her, the girl could sing.

When my stomach rumbled, I bought a Coke and peanut butter

crackers from the machines outside the auditorium. After I swallowed the last cracker, I ran my tongue over my teeth. As I dropped the empty soda can in the trash bin, a hand touched my shoulder.

"Mary, I'm glad to see you. Am I early?" Mrs. Foley asked. Her damp coat smelled of cigarettes and rotten eggs.

"You're a little early, but you can go in. At least you'll get a seat in the front."

I started to move away. Mrs. Foley grabbed my sleeve.

"Connie mentioned she planned to go out with you and Julia after the concert." She reached into her pocket and offered me a handful of crumpled dollars. "I want her to pay her way."

I raised my hands like she pointed a gun. "I don't know anything about that. Maybe Julia asked her." I cleared my throat. "I hardly know Connie. Julia's more her friend."

Mrs. Foley's mouth twitched, and she held her hand to her throat. I was afraid she might collapse in the hallway so I took her arm and led her to a bench outside the auditorium door. Her chest heaved, and she fumbled in her purse for a cigarette. I didn't tell her no smoking was allowed. She exhaled a long stream of smoke and raised her eyes.

"What's wrong with Connie? Why doesn't she have friends?"

I hunched my shoulders and wished I could tuck my head like a turtle. "She's a really good singer," I said.

The school door creaked open, and a cold breeze ruffled my hair. Five junior girls and a junior boy entered the hall, stomping their feet as loud as an avalanche. I wished a wave of snow would knock me down and bury me.

After she dropped her cigarette on the linoleum floor and crushed it with her worn shoe, she moved into the auditorium. As she walked down the aisle, she tapped the end seat on each row. She took a seat three rows from the front. I let out the breath I'd been holding.

I stood against the auditorium's back wall. To Julia's accompaniment, Connie's lively songs delighted the audience. For the finale, Connie sang the Carpenters' song, *Merry Christmas, Darling*. The lyrics — *the lights on my tree, I wish you could see, I wish it every day* — seemed a forlorn message about a life no one wanted to share.

As planned, I waited by the back gym door for Julia. Her shoes tapped down the hall. She rounded the corner with a bouquet of flowers.

"Let's go," she whispered.

Before the door shut behind us, Connie called, "Julia, wait, I want you to meet my mother."

Outside, our breaths rose in pale puffs of steam, and we broke into a run, laughing.

"You were really good," I panted after we reached her car. "Who gave you flowers?"

Julia seemed to notice them for the first time. "Jonathan Mitchell," she said, eyebrows raised in surprise. "He's meeting us at HoJo's." She paused. "He asked me to go ice skating during winter break."

"Jonathan's cute," I said. "Maybe Dominic and I can go skating, too — a double date."

"I'd have to ask Jonathan." Julia's voice was tentative. "I'm not sure Dominic would fit in. He probably doesn't even know how to ice skate. Anyway, I need to get the hell out of here before *Macrobdella* gets her fangs in me again. You coming?"

Wind whistled. I hugged myself. "You go on and meet Jonathan. I better get home."

Julia narrowed her eyes. "I thought we had plans."

"So did Connie," I said.

As I hurried along the sidewalk, my head ached. This time, I couldn't deny Julia's dismissal of Dominic.

"I like him." I said out loud. "I don't care if he fits in with you and Jonathan Mitchell." Something inside my heart tore, like a rag ripping.

A car rumbled, slowed, and pulled over. Connie called out the window, "Hop in. My mom will give you a ride."

"No thanks. I like the night air," I answered, never slowing my pace, never looking her way.

As the car started moving again, I called, "Nice singing."

SATURDAY, Bruno told me to unload crates of pine, fir, and boxwood garlands, then weave some along the shelves. Bruno's hair pomade smelled like butter. He wiped his forehead with a plaid hanky. I wondered if Dominic would look like Bruno in thirty years.

Sticky pine sap oozed from nicks in the garland and gummed up my fingers. After Dominic tied a tree on top of a station wagon filled with kids, he came inside to help. His Santa hat glistened from drizzle, and he blew on his hands to warm them. When I opened my mouth to greet him, I inhaled garland dust, and couldn't stop coughing.

"You gotta stop snorting that stuff, Freckles," Dominic said. "Come on, I'll buy you a Coke."

He wrapped his arm around my shoulders as we headed for the soda machine. Sips of soda soothed my throat, and I sighed. Dominic met my gaze with a crooked smile. Everything about him — his sweat and fresh-bread smell; his clear hazel eyes; his Philly accent; and the way he attacked whatever job Bruno gave him — attracted me, no matter what Julia said about slumming.

As we walked back to the garland display, heat radiated from his body, and my mind filled with anticipation of our first date that night after work. When Connie stepped into our path, I splashed soda all over my apron. Connie glared at Dominic.

"I need to talk to Mary," she said.

Dominic glanced at me, shrugged, and muttered, "I'll get back to the garlands."

"How can I help you?" I asked. A bead of sweat trickled down my back.

"Why do you hate me? Why did you stop being my friend?" Her breath came in short gasps, and her pale eyes turned dark. Her clothes reeked of piss. Her fists clenched.

"I don't hate you, Connie. I barely know you. You're Julia's friend, not mine."

My body trembled, and my stomach lurched. When she stepped toward me, I backed up with my hands raised, waiting for the punch. She stared with dead eyes. I stepped left to walk past her. She blocked my way, face red and mottled.

"It's your fault. Julia said you made her choose. You never liked me."

Her voice sounded a high-pitched alarm. I covered my ears and sensed Dominic's arrival. Connie's shouted accusations — *You made her choose, you never liked me, it's your fault* — faded as Dominic steered her out the door.

I staggered to Bruno's office. He stood in the doorway, eyes sad and kind. I hid behind his stocky frame and leaned my head on his back, breathing the damp wool and cigar smell of his thick work shirt. I stayed that way, trembling, until Dominic joined us.

"She's gone, Mary. I walked her to the bus stop, gave her some change, and told her, never come here again."

"Damn, Freckles, what da hell was dat about?" Bruno swung around and put his hands on my shoulders. "I never seen da likes a dat."

I shook my head to fling off Connie's image.

"You OK ta work?" Bruno asked, voice warm.

"I'll help Mary finish the garlands," Dominic said. "Call me if someone needs a tree."

Somehow, with Dominic at my side, I made it through the day.

After work, Dominic took me to Luigi's for pizza and cokes. In a back booth, he brushed back my hair.

"You're still shaking," he said.

"I can't stop thinking about Connie."

"Forget Connie. She can't force you to be her friend."

Later, in the back seat of his car, I clung to Dominic like I was drowning. His calloused hands caressed my arms, but Connie's accusations thundered in my head. I didn't want to believe Julia said I made her choose between Connie and me, but deep in the pit of my stomach, I knew it was true. Dominic's kisses drew my thoughts to him.

After he walked me to the door, I lingered on the porch until his car's lights disappeared from view.

Monday morning, a light snow dusted the ground, and I wished I'd worn boots for the walk to school. With my head and shoulders hunched against the bitter cold I didn't notice Julia until I reached the school's concrete steps. She grabbed my sleeve, and we entered the building together.

"Mary, I've been waiting for you. Now that the concert's over we can get back to normal."

It felt good to walk down the hall shoulder to shoulder with Julia. I denied the terrible thoughts Connie put in my head. My heart beat with hope. After I stowed my spattered ski jacket in my locker, we headed to the study room to talk before class.

"Did you know Connie came to the Garden Center on Saturday?" I asked.

Julia's eyes widened. "How would I know that?"

"She was horrible, Julia. She screamed at me." I gazed at Julia's intelligent eyes and concerned smile. Connie's words came to me. "Did you tell Connie I made you choose?"

"Choose what?" Julia's eyes flitted side to side. She rubbed a finger behind her ear.

I opened my mouth, but the first bell rang, and we gathered our books. In English, we sat next to each other but averted our eyes.

I fought tears all morning, but in the cafeteria, Julia waved for me to sit with her like always, and helped herself to my chips.

"We're fine, right? Best friends?" she asked.

"Best friends," I agreed.

But as hard as I tried, as much as I hoped, I couldn't ignore the ache in my heart.

Christmas Eve, the Garden Center closed at 4:00. Dominic promised to visit my home Christmas afternoon to meet my family.

Julia invited me to her Christmas Eve piano concert at the Episcopal Church. I changed into black slacks and tucked in the white silk blouse my mother found at Bargain Basement. As I leaned toward the mirror to dab on mascara, the phone rang.

"Mary." Julia's short, sharp breaths sounded like sobs.

"What's wrong?" I asked, fearful and confused.

"It's Connie," she said.

Rage coursed through me. I visualized Connie screaming at Julia like she yelled at me.

"Mary, are you there?" Julia's voice was small and tight.

"What did she do?" I took a deep breath and allowed my hatred to simmer.

"God, it's horrible. She was supposed to sing with the Church choir tonight, but her mother found her with a needle jammed in her arm and a jug of insecticide spilled on floor. Her face was swollen and purple. She killed herself, Mary."

I pictured Connie sprawled on the floor alongside the jug of Annihilator I sold her. "I can't talk about this," I said and hung up.

Deltamethrin. Do not touch, inhale, or ingest. Keep away from children and pets. Get it at the Garden Center.

I went to the bathroom and puked.

TWO DAYS AFTER CHRISTMAS, Connie's funeral was held at the Episcopal Church. Julia begged me to go with her, and my dad let me borrow his car to drive to the service. I parked around the corner, out of sight. In the chilly morning air, I walked to an ancient oak tree at the edge of the church lawn. From behind the tree, I watched elderly women toddle up stone steps and move through the ornate wooden doors. I shivered and stomped my feet on the damp carpet of fallen leaves.

Soon, Julia drove into the parking lot, solemnly climbed the steps, and entered the church. I knew she waited inside, but like Lot's wife, when I looked back at the gallon of death I sold Connie, I became a pillar of salt. Still, Connie found me. *You never liked me. It's your fault. You made Julia choose . . .*

With my forehead pressed against the rough bark, I shielded myself from gusts of wind until the doors opened, and mourners descended the steps. In the parking lot, a man in a black overcoat waved cars into line behind the hearse. Julia's yellow Camaro was a bright spot among the dark Fords and Chevys. After the last car turned out of sight, I drove my father's car to the cemetery but parked in a shopping center across the highway. Along the path winding through the graves, I followed the sound of Mrs. Foley's sorrowful wails to the tiny group shivering near the chain-link fence that marked the graveyard boundary.

I stopped at another family's gravesite, too far away for Connie's mourners to notice me. Connie's coffin was suspended over her grave, next to a mound of dirt. On the other side of the chain-link fence, cars and trucks roared along the busy road. Before the casket descended into the grave, Mrs. Foley's keening turned my blood to ice. I stumbled away on quivering legs.

~

AN HOUR LATER, I answered the phone.

"I waited for you. Why didn't you come?" Julia asked.

"I was there," I answered. "Alone."

I listened to her quiet breathing. I wanted her to say, I understand, Mary. None of this was your fault.

Instead, she sighed and said, "I don't know what's gotten into you, or why you changed. I don't know who you are anymore. I just know you're not my friend Mary."

I hung up and wandered outside. In the chill wind, my ears ached, and my teeth chattered. I welcomed the pain.

As 1975 withered and died, I buried my dreams of fine clothes, nice cars, and privilege. I knew who I was.

~

FORTY YEARS LATER, I study Julia as she studies me. Her white hair ages her. Ravages from sun, stress, and time mark both our faces. The girls we were are long gone. We struggle for something to say.

"Do you still play piano?" I ask.

"I chair the Music Department at Chestnut Hill College. My daughter's a member of the Juilliard String Quartet. What about you? After high school you disappeared."

"Dominic and I moved to Maryland. He owns a home renovation business, and our son works with him. One daughter's a physical therapist, the other teaches high school English. I write about gardening. I'm here to do research."

I unwind the paper edging on the rim of my coffee cup. Julia folds and refolds a paper napkin. I long to broach the subject of Connie, but it was too long ago. We share glimpses of our lives but hide our desperation. Before she rises to leave, she writes her email address on a napkin, and the letters bleed into the creases.

"Stay in touch," she says in the breezy way I remember, and turns to go.

"We're moving back in the spring," I call.

My breath catches at the warmth of her smile.

I PULL out my cell phone and check my appointments, then call Dominic and tell him I'll be home tonight. I straighten my notes and slide them in my briefcase. The early afternoon sun shines bright this unusually warm December day. I drive to the Garden Center — now called Green Stuff — and snap a photo to text to Dominic.

Inside, an unimaginably young girl stands at the register scrolling through her iPhone. I pay for my purchase with cash, and she cracks her gum as she hands me my change.

I drive to the cemetery and park my car near the entrance. My parents, dead for so many years, rest in this very cemetery in the beautifully kept section I chose, with a statue of Gabriel to guard their tombs. Names on tombstones read like a grade school class roster: Rooney, O'Neil, Romano, Cataldi, and Beebe, who died at thirteen. As I wander along the winding paths, the wind blows up my hair like a sail.

On the highway a truck blasts its horn. I hop over graves, trying to respect the dead, but they're clustered too close to avoid. Along the chain-link fence, I examine flat granite markers until finally I find a sunken stone chiseled with the name Constance C. Foley, 1960-1975, and below it, Margaret M. Foley, 1928-1996. Grass grows in irregular patches, and chunks of dirt from a fresh grave lie like spattered insults across the depressed length of the plot.

I kneel on the damp earth and dig my fingers in the ill-tended spongy soil. I remember the sad, lonely girl buried here, her casket crushed under the weight of her mother's more recent demise. A breeze chills me, and I place a hand on the marker to steady myself as I rise. I vow to return in the spring when the crocus bulbs I planted on Connie's grave rise up in glory. I move to where I watched that day, too cowardly to acknowledge the life I disregarded.

Across the stunning blue sky, clouds shaped like ships crash and drift over churning seas.

As I walk away, my footsteps tap a solemn cadence on the cracked concrete path, and I fight the urge to turn back.

2

PIECE MAN

S ummer is over. Without regret, I lock the door to my art gallery for the last time. Let fortune's wheel spin someone else, someone young, to forge her future in this boardwalk shop. All I take with me is one drawing —*Piece Man.* In it, shallow waves break along the shoreline. A seagull glides over the dark ocean, fading into the pale horizon. A boy, arms spread like wings in flight, stands in stark contrast to the dead colors of that dead day. I remember well it was April, more than thirty years ago.

Three nights before, my husband told me it was over. Now that our daughter was grown, he was done with the charade. He'd make certain I'd have enough money. He just wanted out. Heartsick, I grabbed paints, pencils, and sketchbooks, and drove a hundred miles to the Jersey shore. Despite the offseason, I found a cottage to rent. After two days drinking expensive wine and staring at an ancient television, I forced myself to go outside.

As I teetered toward the waves, wind whistled like a far-off train, drowning the sounds of the sea. Squawking seagulls darted at the remains of a crab. In the wet sand, my footprints washed away and disappeared.

With bare feet numbed by the lick of waves, I walked until the rocks of a jetty loomed before me. A small boy balanced on the biggest rock. Though the air was frigid, he wore no shirt. His arms spread outward and his ribs protruded under winter-white skin. Cropped blond hair framed a chiseled face. Graffiti covered the rock — spray-painted signatures of persons unknown. In thick white letters someone painted, **Piece Man.** I followed the child's gaze to the sea.

"Hey," I called, "what are you doing up there?"

The boy turned. "I'm looking for my mother."

"Is she in the ocean?" My voice trembled.

"Before she died on Sunday, Mom said whenever I need her, come to the ocean, lift up my arms, and she'll be there."

"It's hard to lose someone you love," I said.

The boy jumped down, recklessly close to the pointy rocks.

"Are you OK?" I asked.

"Why do you care?"

"I lost my husband Sunday."

"Did he tell you to come here, too?"

"No, I figured that out myself."

The boy's features softened. "It's better for them, you know. My brother says they're not suffering anymore."

He turned and ran across the sand to a car parked along the road. An older boy, his brother I supposed, leaned against a dented Mustang. As they drove away, the brother honked the horn.

At the cottage, my pencil, moving on its own, formed images on page after page. The vision of the boy on the jetty tormented me, demanding the perfect depiction. Finally, I could do no more.

I never returned to the city. I bought the cottage and opened my boardwalk gallery. *Piece Man* hung on the wall, but was never for sale. Tonight, I'll walk along the shore.

3

ORIGINAL SINS

Frank Dominico parked his black SUV on the crumbling asphalt driveway of the home he ran away from thirty-three years ago. Outside, he stuck his hands in his pockets and hunched his shoulders against the chilly March air. As he circled the stone house his family moved into the year he turned four, he noticed cracks in the mortar. He pried out a loose chip, then replaced it. Frank remembered his father telling him the house was built in 1897 of Wissahickon schist. The glittery stones of Philadelphia made him weep for the life he abandoned. He wiped his eyes and gazed at the horizon, where the morning sun cast a dull glow through clusters of clouds.

As he returned to the front of the house, his heart raced. A copper-colored minivan pulled in behind his SUV. Maria. Would he recognize his sister? When he ran away, she was sixteen. Now, she was almost fifty. Frank wondered what she'd think of him, with grey hair and a bald spot expanding on his crown. At fifty-one, the slender body he carried away from home had become thickset, and he feared she'd recoil from the scar that split the left side of his ruddy face. He walked across the overgrown front yard and opened the minivan door.

"Maria?" His voice cracked. "Maria?"

A sharp-featured woman with high cheekbones, a perfect nose, and smooth olive skin stepped out and gazed at him from Maria's deep brown eyes, filled with tears. They stared at each other, speechless, before embracing.

"Frankie?" The woman who was his little sister shook her head. "God damn you, Frankie."

"You look good, Maria." Instead of the sweet kid sister he imagined all these years, Maria seemed fierce.

"What happened to you, Frankie?" She ran a finger over his scar. "What happened to your face?"

He shrugged. "Shrapnel. I was lucky. My buddy lost his arm and his hearing. Happened a long time ago."

"You should have told us, Frankie. We worried about you. Postcards a few times a year, phone calls at Christmas — that wasn't enough. You drive up today?" She blew out a breath like she was exhaling cigarette smoke.

"Last night. I got a room at the Fort Washington Hotel. Driving here along Bethlehem Pike felt surreal. Some places look the same, some are completely different. Your kids in school?"

"Like I told you on the phone, Mikey's away at college. Teresa and Lucy are at Springfield High. Come to dinner tonight. Mike will be there and you'll meet the girls. The place is a mess. After Pops died, Ma didn't let anyone in the house but me. I tried to keep up, but I have my own home. You should have come to see her, Frankie."

"She hated me, Maria. She didn't want me here," he said.

Sadness, guilt, and dread washed over him, the feelings that drove him away. He took a deep breath. You're goddamned fifty-one years old, he told himself. Get a grip. Don't embarrass yourself.

"You should have come for Pops. You should have come for me."

Maria reached into the back of her car and pulled out plastic storage bins. Frank took them and followed her. She stopped at the rusty wrought iron gate to Ma's Mary garden. The gate screeched open over the concrete walk. On the right, tiny bursts of purple, yellow, and white emerged amid weeds in the garden their mother nurtured to honor the mother of Christ. Vines crawled over the bench Pops built for Ma to sit on while she worshipped. From a spalled concrete pedestal, the Virgin Mary gazed down. Delicate dirt lines creased her face. Patches of blue dotted her robes. Frank shivered.

Maria moved to the porch steps. "Watch yourself. The second step's broken."

Frank steadied himself on the handrail. Rust flakes stuck to his palm. He wanted to ask Maria why she allowed the house to deteriorate like this, but when he looked in her narrowed eyes, he choked back his words.

"Yikes," he said instead.

He mentally calculated the supplies and time he'd need to fix the step. The boss gave him the week off to take care of family business. Frank figured he'd need it.

Maria opened the dark walnut door. Inside smelled dusty and dead. A nativity stable with Jesus, Mary, Joseph, wise men, shepherds, camels, and lambs decorated the top of the old piano. Sheet music — *Immaculate Mary, our hearts are on fire* — curled on the piano rack.

"Before we get started, we need to talk," Maria said. "Ma didn't keep coffee, but I can make tea."

She passed through the living room into the dining room and entered the kitchen. Frank set the bins by the front staircase.

"I'll be there in a minute. Everything's the same. It's weird."

A red oriental rug, now faded and worn, covered the living room floor. Frank remembered tracing the floral pattern with his finger then drawing the pattern along the border of his copybook. The next day, when the nun at Holy Ghost Elementary checked his homework, she slapped a ruler across his palm for defiling the pages. His hand burned at the memory.

The shelves of the bookcase Pops built held legions of saints. Frank counted thirty-seven statues. Like an annoying song he couldn't get out of his head, the litany of the saints from his altar boy days looped through his mind — *Saint Peter, Saint Paul, Saint Andrew, Saint James, Saint John, Saint Thomas, Saint Philip, Saint Bartholomew* . . . Before he got to *pray for us*, the tea kettle whistle broke his reverie.

He joined his sister in the kitchen, where they sat in their childhood places. Frank swore he smelled tomato gravy and garlic. He worked on a spot on the table with his fingernail.

"You broke Pops' heart when you took off and joined the army, Frankie. The first year you were gone, he raced to the phone each time it rang, sure it was you. After we got your postcard from Fort Jackson, Pops watched TV every night, making Ma and me shut up for any Army news, especially when troops were sent overseas — the Middle East, Panama, Africa. He prayed for you, Frankie — *God protect my son*. He blamed himself that you went away."

Maria dipped her tea bag, and the water grew dark in her cup. Frank rubbed his sore left knee. At least Maria couldn't see the burn scars on his chest and legs.

He stared into his cup. "What about Ma?"

Maria caught the teabag and set it on the saucer. She took a sip, then let out a sigh and a sad laugh.

"Ma prayed to her saints. She went to Mass. A year after you left, she got a job at the rectory cooking and cleaning for the priests. Since she couldn't give God her only son, she figured the least she could do was serve his anointed." Again Maria exhaled like a smoker.

Frank guessed she gave up cigarettes only recently. He tipped his head to take in his sister. He wished he could travel back in time like the Superman movie he saw when he was thirteen. He imagined Maria in the living room, dressed for senior prom, waiting for Mike McCarthy. He visualized dancing with her at her wedding to *Landslide* by Fleetwood Mac. The image of the baptismal font came to mind, with Maria holding her first born, Michael, while Frank, garbed in priestly vestments, dripped water on the baby's forehead and blessed him . . . *and of the Holy Spirit*. Frank dropped his cup.

"What, Frankie, what? You look sick. Get up before tea spills all over your pants."

While Maria sloshed a rag across the table, Frank knelt to pick up the shattered porcelain.

"She convinced me I was the chosen one," he said from the floor. He hoisted himself up, dropped the pieces in the trash can, swept his hand in a wide arc, and made the sign of the cross. "In the name of the mother, the son, and the holy statues."

"Amen," Maria said from the sink. She squeezed the rag and draped it over the faucet. "Remember you used to put grape juice in the brandy snifter and made me stick out my tongue to receive oyster crackers? Ma told everyone, 'My Frankie's gonna be a priest.'"

"Ma was relentless. Even after Pops told her . . ." Frank stopped. Of course Maria didn't know. He didn't want her to know.

He cleared his throat. "It wasn't fair to leave like that, but I had to get out of here to save my soul."

"What about my soul? You left me, too, Frankie, and I was too young to save myself. You think a few lousy postcards and five-minute phone calls at Christmas made up for leaving me? I needed you. You didn't even come home when Pops died." Maria's voice trembled with rage, and her eyes grew cold. She slammed her fist on the table. "I had to hire a fucking private detective to find you to tell you Ma died."

"For Christ's sake, Maria, when Pops died I was fighting in Iraq. I couldn't get home," Frank said. He closed his eyes and told himself to keep his voice down. "I'm sorry I didn't let you know when I moved to Norfolk. I planned to call as soon as I got settled. Before I got the job installing cable for Comcast, I crashed with different Army buddies. When your investigator found me, I'd just moved into my own apartment. I was going to call."

"That's goddamned not good enough, Frank. You went off and did whatever the hell you pleased while I stayed here, the dutiful daughter, the supportive wife, the loving mother. How could you not care about me? Did you even think about me?" Maria stared out the kitchen window, trembling.

"I thought about you every day, Maria." He moved to her side. She smelled like Philly — of thick crusty bread, onions and peppers, red wine, and tomatoes. "I thought you hated me."

Maria's face softened. With smudged mascara, she looked like a kid playing with makeup — the little sister he left behind. Frank's eyes rose to the windowsill and unconsciously, he inched back. She followed his gaze to the small statue of a green-robed woman with a lizard nestled at her feet. She wiped her eyes, raised an eyebrow, and allowed a tight smile to cross her lips.

"Saint Martha, patron of cooks and housewives. Ma said she tamed a dragon with holy water."

"Too bad Saint Martha didn't tame Ma." Frank took a breath. "Give me a chance, Maria. I missed you. I missed Pops and Ma. I missed this house, but I couldn't come home."

Maria punched Frank hard in his left arm, his injured side. He sucked in his breath but didn't flinch. He tightened his gut, ready for her flailing fists.

"Go ahead, Maria. I deserve it. But I promise to do better."

Maria stood stiff as a statue, her face a mask. "We'll see, Frankie. Anyway, the attorney says we gotta go through all this crap and agree on who gets what. After that, I'll hire people to get rid of the rest of the stuff, make repairs, clean, and paint before we show it for sale."

"You're going to sell the house?" Frank followed her out of the kitchen through the dining room and living room to the staircase.

"What, you want to buy it?"

"Just asking."

He couldn't imagine other people living here. All those years, all the places he lived, he never belonged. This was his only home.

At the bottom of the stairs, Frank grabbed the plastic bins, and joined Maria, who stood on the landing next to her life-sized namesake. A hint of a smile crossed Maria Goretti's finely chiseled face. Maria Goretti, child saint, eleven-year-old Italian peasant girl who bitterly fought off her attacker in an unsuccessful attempt to preserve her virginity — and died of fourteen stab wounds. Frank's eyes met Maria's, and they laughed like they did the day Ma made Frank help Pops carry Maria Goretti from the station wagon into the house.

"If Pops hadn't rigged up the wheelbarrow, I'd have popped my balls when we moved her." Frank sneezed at the plaster smell.

"After you got her upright, Ma made us kneel on the step and pray. *Heroic and angelic Saint Maria Goretti, we kneel before thee to honor thy persevering fortitude and to beg thy gracious aid,*" Maria said. "Even now I can't walk past without crossing myself."

"I doubt you still need divine intervention to protect your virginity."

A warm feeling rushed through him. Despite years apart, his love for his sister felt stronger than ever. He hoped she felt it, too.

On the wall along the stairwell, flowered wallpaper curled at the seams. With each footstep, the creaky stairs sounded like a childhood song. Upstairs, the air smelled stale. A few steps ahead, Maria bent over, coughing. She patted her pocket, pulled out a yellow squirt gun, and pressed it between her lips — an inhaler. Frank watched with sad eyes. He knew so little about her life — only that she married Mike, had three children, and lived a few miles from here. And she knew nothing of his. How much of each other's torments could they bear?

Eyes watery, Maria said, "After I got pneumonia last winter, the asthma got worse."

WHEN HE ENTERED the second-floor hallway, Frank felt bewildered, even drunk. He put his hand against the wall to stay upright. Spots floated in his vision. Last week, after Maria called and he agreed to come home, he knew it would be hard. He'd have to control his temper and bite his tongue. He never anticipated shock. Outside the door to his childhood bedroom, he caught his breath. He felt trapped, as if he were under enemy fire. The plastic bins slipped from his hand.

"Frankie? You need to sit down? Look at the two of us — Ma still brings us to our knees."

With gratitude and a weak smile, Frank steadied his breath and studied his sister. The two of us, she'd said, like when they were kids.

"We won't let her," he said.

Before he pushed open his bedroom door, he glanced at Maria, and nodded to the bins.

"Sure, sure, take what you need. You go on. I'm gonna collect what I want from my old room. You OK?"

"I'm good." Maybe he was.

Dust motes sprang from the tan corduroy cover when Frank sat on his bed. The window was jammed shut, but with a couple whacks, he lifted it a few inches. The fresh air smelled like wet leaves.

On the shelf above his old bureau, brown-robed Saint Francis of Assisi stood on sandaled feet with a dusty lamb at his side, and a dove perched on his outstretched arm. The metal plate on the base read — *Go, Francis, and repair my house, which as you see is falling into ruin.*

"You got that right, Brother Francis," he said.

His bureau drawers were empty except for his high school baseball uniform. He dropped it in a bin and wondered why his parents saved it. He turned to the closet. Three hatboxes from Roxborough Millinery sat on the shelf above the clothes rod. Dust and dry insects spilled on his head when he pulled them down. He brushed off the boxes and set them on the bed. They smelled like old books.

Pops' suits, dress shirts, slacks, and coat hung on the closet rod. He supposed Ma moved them here after Pops died. Frank wished he could have come home for Pops' funeral, but he was near dead himself, 2,175 miles from Baghdad in the U.S. Army hospital in Landstuhl, Germany. Along with shrapnel wounds, his left side — arm, leg, and torso — sustained deep second-degree burns, and black stitches held his cheek together. 'Don't notify my family,' he insisted before the morphine kicked in. 'I'll tell them myself.'

Frank checked Pops' pockets and found thirty-seven crisp dollars. Next to the old camel hair coat, a dry cleaner bag protected white and red garments. His stomach lurched, and his mind raced. He wanted to hide them. No, he wanted to destroy the red cassock and white surplice, the altar boy vestments Father Smitty gave him to keep. Before he jammed them in a trash bag, Maria's footsteps drew close.

She called from the hallway, "Frankie?"

"In here."

She squeezed past, shoved the hatboxes aside, and sat on the bed. The vestments swung from his upstretched hand.

"Ma kept your altar boy clothes? No way."

Frank hung the vestments in the closet. "I guess she didn't know how to get rid of them. I think they have to be burned or buried, like the American flag."

"I can't believe you know that. Maybe you really should have been a priest."

"Instead, I was a soldier of God. Or the United States Army. One or the other."

Maria's familiar laugh tore away the tendrils of shame that tightened around his heart whenever he recalled his childhood aspiration. He wanted that memory to burn with his vestments.

While Frank rummaged through shoes on the closet floor, Maria opened the hatboxes. One held their father's fedora. She tossed it like a Frisbee, and Frank set it on his head, grateful for Maria's presence. He hoped she didn't notice his trembling hands.

"You look good, Frankie, like *Mad Men*. God, look at these pictures."

As if she were dealing a deck of cards, Maria flicked photos into piles on the bed. Frank moved to the window, away from the chemical smell of old photographs. He took a deep breath before the quiet swish of the pictures beckoned as if calling his name.

"What's the name of that priest in all these pictures?" Maria asked. "He had a funny name, right?"

"Father Smith." Frank stared at the photo of himself in altar boy vestments with the handsome young priest's arm around his shoulders. "We called him Father Smitty." He wanted to crumple the photo, but tossed it back.

Maria sorted through other photos and sneezed. "Damn, Frankie, you were the golden boy. There's hardly any pictures of me."

The golden boy. The boy destined for the priesthood. The boy who served Mass before school in the morning, and stayed after to prepare the altar for the next day. The boy who memorized his missal, who bowed his head in prayer each night before bed and dreamed of ringing bells — da ding, da ding, da ding. The boy Father Smitty called blessed. The boy who loved Father Smitty above all else.

"Frankie, here's a picture of you and Father Smitty on the Ferris wheel at the church carnival. You look so happy," Maria said. "He liked you, didn't he?"

"He liked me so much the new pastor sent him away."

FRANK WAS eleven years old the day he vowed to Father Smitty he'd become a priest. Father led him to the small chapel in the rectory, filled the chalice with wine, raised it, and said, 'Francis, do you willingly and knowingly choose to partake in the sacraments of secret communion and sacred love, and vow to honor the solemnity of silence all the days of your life?'

Frank, trembling with desire, answered, 'Yes, Father.'

Father Smitty held out the chalice. 'Sacred love is never jealous, never boastful. It does not seek its own advantage, nor take offense, nor store up grievances. It protects the beloved and endures whatever comes. Is it by your free will you take up this cup?'

Frank longed for holiness. His soul cried out for the sacraments of secret communion and sacred love. 'Yes, Father,' he said, and swallowed the sour wine.

After he emptied the chalice, Father handed him an altar cloth to wipe his lips.

Then Father told him to pray with him — *When I was a child, I spoke as a child, and saw things as a child, and thought like a child; but now I am a man and I put away my childish ways.* Is it time to put away your childish ways, Francis?"

'Yes, Father,' Frank answered.

There in the rectory chapel, Father Smitty sat in the last pew, took Frank onto his lap, and held him close. Against Frank's back, Father Smitty's chest felt warm and strong. His gentle caresses thundered in Frank's brain, and he experienced the rapture of sacred love. Even now he heard Father Smitty's soft words, 'Sacred love must never be taken, Francis, it must be given with kindness and accepted with joy. Do you accept with joy, Francis?'

To his shame, Frank accepted with joy for six years, doubt dispelled by rapture, until the Sunday afternoon he climbed out the rectory window and found Pops waiting.

Before the IED blast, nothing hurt him more than Pops' fists on his face and his words in his ears — 'I'm ashamed to call you my son.'

FRANK'S ENTIRE BODY TREMBLED. A warm hand cradled his, and he turned into Maria's embrace.

She rocked and whispered, "I never knew, Frankie. I'm sorry. If I'd known, I'd . . ."

Frank's trembling turned to shaky laughter. He pulled back, gazed at his sister, and touched her cheek.

"You were a kid, Maria. You couldn't help me." He took a deep breath. "The worst thing is, I didn't want to be helped. I believed everything Father Smitty said. He told me Jesus Christ gave priests a secret sacrament of love they only shared with boys who promised to become priests and took the solemn vow of silence. I never broke that solemn vow, not even when Pops tried to beat it out of me, until now."

"Oh my God, Frankie. The man used you. He stole your childhood," Maria said.

Frank couldn't meet her eyes. "I gave it away."

"That man is a criminal. He needs to go to jail. He needs to pay for what he did to you. You should sue," she said, enraged.

"He paid for his sins. After Pops figured out what was going on and told the pastor, Father Smith went away. I was a mess. I didn't know who or what to believe. I didn't know who I was supposed to be." Frank shook his head. "The day Pops told me Father Smith drove his car off a bridge, I ran away."

Frank felt so tired. He'd exhausted his rage during thirty years carrying a gun. Sure, shame and humiliation crept into his dreams. But he read a lot about pedophilia. He studied victims' accounts, and studied articles about priests brought to justice after decades of cover-up. He knew the abuse wasn't his fault. He'd been a vulnerable child manipulated by a man who swore their love was blessed. Frank put his hands on Maria's shoulders and looked in his sister's eyes.

Maria said, "We'll get you help."

"Father Smith stole my innocence. He manipulated me, and abused his power. I was so pissed about that for so long, I got no piss left." He sighed. "I'm mostly OK. A long time ago, I forgave myself. What I never got over all these years is the way he obliterated my destiny. I was supposed to be a priest. I never considered any other future. I'd make Ma proud, I'd say Mass and bless the unfortunate. When Father Smith destroyed my dream, he left me with nothing and no place to go." He kissed Maria's cheek. "God, I missed you. I missed having a home, a place where I belong."

"You didn't have to run away. Sure, Pops and Ma had problems, but they loved you, Frankie. They could have saved you."

"You don't get it, Maria. You don't have a goddamned clue what it was like for me." Frank's scar throbbed. "A week after Pops beat me, he and Ma had a terrible fight. Pops yelled, 'I won't let that boy spend another minute with a priest. It's not normal, for Christ's sake.' Ma slammed a frying pan on the table and shouted, 'My son will be a priest, Joe. You have no say.' Pops shoved her, and her head hit the wall. Pops stormed out yelling, 'You and your goddamned priests.'"

Maria recoiled. "Why did you let it go on so long? At some point you had to know it was wrong."

"It was easy for you. No one expected you to be anything. I was supposed to be a priest. My life was supposed to mean something." Frank flushed, his nostrils flared, his hands clenched in fists. He wanted to slap her.

"You go to hell." Maria pushed past him and stomped down the stairs.

The front door opened then slammed shut.

FRANK ENTERED MARIA'S BEDROOM, where Saint Anthony stood on the corner shelf Pops built, to watch the minivan back out of the driveway and speed down the road. I should go, too, he thought. This was a mistake. My life is one mistake after the other.

Years ago, when he lay wounded in the hospital, he promised himself he'd find a woman, marry, settle down, live a normal life, maybe have a couple kids. Instead, after months of rehab he re-upped and redeployed. He went wherever they sent him and did whatever they told him to do. It was easy that way. But when he reached thirty years, his major ordered him to make plans for civilian life.

God, he loved Maria. The short time they'd been together wrapped him in a warm blanket of belonging he'd almost forgotten. He'd finish up here then call her, say he's sorry for being a jerk.

Still, with Maria gone, he felt lighter. He wanted to dig through his bedroom closet, and he wanted to do it without her sad eyes and angry words, without wallowing in the pit in his heart he spent thirty years trying to fill.

WHEN HE CROUCHED to search the closet, sharp pain shot through his knee. He left the *Advil* at the hotel. Screw it, he thought, I've had worse pain. He pushed aside the neatly lined-up shoes to reach the cut-out access to bathroom pipes. The cover opened easily. Frank fumbled for his cell phone, and tapped the flashlight app.

A shadowy shape emerged in the dim light. He slid out a dust-covered cardboard box. This box played in his dreams. He often worried that rodents gnawed away the pages, or water seeped in and ruined every book. He dusted off the top and opened it. Inside his comic books waited, each one in a plastic cover supported by a cardboard slat.

"Maria, they're here, just like I left them."

He wished his little sister were here to share this treasure. She would know how much they meant to him.

Frank wanted to carry the comics to his car, drive away, and never come back. But he needed to go through the house, into their parents' bedroom, remember better days, then clean up for dinner with his sister and her family.

He looked forward to seeing Maria's home, get to know Mike again, and meet his nieces. He wanted to tell Teresa and Lucy about the places he'd been. After the girls went to do homework or text their friends, he needed to talk to Maria and Mike about the woman he met in Norfolk. He wanted to know what they thought about him seeing a thirty-eight-year-old woman with two little girls and a dog named Rascal.

As he transferred the comics from the deteriorating cardboard box into a plastic bin, Frank thought about the cheap dives he'd slept in and the sorry women he'd picked up. He made promises he planned never to keep, and checked out as soon as a woman wanted more than he had to give — until he knocked on Rosie's apartment door a month ago. While he replaced her set-top box and installed a new Internet modem, her four-year-old twin girls asked him a million questions.

"What happened to your face? Does it hurt? Can we touch it?"

When Rosie apologized, he told her he loved kids and hers were great. She offered him a cup of coffee, and he accepted. They talked until the dispatcher called to say his next customer was waiting. It took him a week to screw up the courage to knock on the door and ask Rosie and the girls to lunch at McDonalds. Since then, they'd gone out for ice cream and on walks in the park with Rascal.

But Frank didn't know how to take the next step, or if he should. Maybe he didn't deserve a nice girl like Rosie, maybe he was too old for her. Maria would know — if she ever spoke to him again.

His stomach growled, and he checked the time — a little after noon.

As FRANK ARRANGED hat boxes and comics in the back of his SUV, Maria's minivan crunched into the driveway. He felt shy, like a damned fool, but met Maria as she climbed out of her car.

"You're such an ass, Frankie. I don't know why I care about you." She opened the back door. "Grab those bags, will you?"

"I got my comics, Maria. They're all there, in pretty good shape. I'm going to read every one."

"You loved them, Frankie. I bet they're worth a bundle. That's so great," she said, her tone honest and forgiving.

Tears welled in his eyes. "I'm sorry, Maria. I've been carrying that weight all my life, but I didn't need to dump it on you." He was sobbing, deep wretched sobs, loud enough for the neighbors to hear.

"Come inside, Frankie. You're home, back in the crazy house."

The bags emitted the satisfying hoagie scent of oil, onions, oregano, and fresh bread. Occasionally over the years he'd eaten a sub, slice of pizza, cheese steak, or soft pretzel that reminded him of Philly, but none smelled like this.

They sat again at the kitchen table. Olive oil blossomed on doubled white paper plates, and shreds of lettuce and onions spilled from the rolls. Frank savored each bite, especially the roll with its crusty outside and chewy inside — the perfect cradle for capicola, Genoa salami, pepper ham, and provolone tucked around lettuce, tomatoes, and strings of red onion sprinkled with olive oil and oregano. When he glanced at Maria, he smiled, ready to listen.

"After you left, Pops got all anxious and crazy — checking the news, running for the phone, shaking out magazines in case your post card got trapped in the pages. Ma became a total religious fanatic freak. I swear, she wore a rosary around her neck. Once I asked why she prayed so much, and she got major pissed. She said because she sinned. I told her go to confession and get forgiveness. 'Frankie was my absolution, and now he's gone,' she said. Do you believe that crap? Looney tunes. I married Mike after high school, just to get away."

"We had good times, too, didn't we, Maria? When our friends came over for dinner, Ma sang while she cooked — *Jimmy Mack, when are you coming back?* At my baseball games, she and Pops sat in the top row. All the way in the outfield, I'd hear her yelling, 'Get the ball, Frankie. Throw it to third.' Remember she loved the Wildwood boardwalk and the tilt-a-whirl? Where did all that go?" Frank shook his head and popped the last bit of hoagie in his mouth.

"I don't know, Frankie. I think it went with you." Maria gathered the trash and shoved it in a plastic bag. "This stuff will stink if we leave it here. Don't let me forget it."

"What now?"

Frank swished his Coke and swallowed the last drops. He rarely drank soda, but today it tasted perfect.

Maria wiped her hands and tugged her ear. Frank liked grown-up Maria. When he agreed to come home he expected her to be softer, maybe chubby, certainly less fierce.

"We have to go through the papers in their bedroom," she said.

"I found thirty-seven bucks in Pops' pockets." Frank flicked the wad on the table. "Give it to the girls."

When they passed Maria Goretti, her eyes held Frank's. He nodded, then steeled himself for their parents' bedroom. But instead of anger and resentment, melancholy pierced his heart. He remembered when he and Maria took sick, Ma tucked them in the big bed surrounded with pillows, and fed them homemade chicken soup.

In the Army hospital, Frank dreamt the hand on his forehead was his mother's. He woke up calling for her. The nurse was kind. 'We all need our mothers when we're hurt,' she told him. Maybe it was true.

The bed was stripped, with the mattress encased in plastic. A wooden cane dangled from the headboard. Frank took Ma's missal from the nightstand. Its cracked leather cover smelled like incense. He felt Maria's eyes on him and returned the book. When he glanced at Ma's dresser, his cheeks burned.

On the dresser top, twelve candle holders that looked like shot glasses held burned-down votive candles with crisp black wicks. Dust coated Mary Magdalene, who knelt on one knee, reaching for a spilled jug. Her face turned up in surprise, as if caught in a sin. A parade of saints joined the Magdalene. Some Frank recognized — Joseph with his staff, Sebastian pierced by arrows, Teresa with a book in hand, dark-skinned Martin de Porres, John Bosco with a school boy, and the tallest statue, Francis of Assisi with a wolf by his side.

Frank, eyebrow raised, turned to Maria. "Ma loved Saint Francis."

"She put statues of him all over the house." She puffed out a breath. "What on earth are we going to do with them?"

"Burn them?" Frank's smile was grim.

Behind the Magdalene, Frank found a red box of kitchen matches. Inside, most of the match sticks were cracked. He pictured his mother's gnarled fingers gripping a match, sliding it across the strike surface without success, then dropping it back in the box. He took a match and struck it. The sulfury smell brought the memory of striking matches beside the altar and praying the tall candle wicks lit up. The tiny flame burned his fingertip. He dropped the match on a candle.

Maria held out her hand. Frank placed the match box in her palm. With a tiny spurt of smoke, a match head snapped aflame. She lit a candle, then another, then a third before she blew it out.

"I feel like we should slide quarters in a slot and kneel to pray," Maria said. "God, Ma loved to light candles."

"The things she believed. The things she made me believe." Frank looked in his sister's eyes as the flames burned yellow and the melting wax smell filled the room. "Why?"

"I don't know, Frankie. I guess she needed to." Maria exhaled in the smoker way and tugged on a dresser drawer. "How about I go through Ma's bureau while you look through the papers? They kept them in a laundry basket in the closet."

FRANK DRAGGED out the laundry basket and set it beside a torn footrest, its flowered fabric faded and dull. When he sat on it, it released a putrid smell like ancient vomit.

The first envelope was marked *Frankie* in red magic marker. As soon as he realized what it contained, he started to call Maria over but changed his mind. Later at her house, he'd show her and the girls his construction-paper drawings, elementary school worksheets, and the school photos Ma and Pops kept all these years. As he sorted through the envelope, he noticed Ma organized them in chronological order, starting before kindergarten. She loved me once, he thought. She saved all this stuff because she loved me. He imagined Ma pulling out the laundry basket from time to time to stare at these childhood mementos, and wondered what she thought as she contemplated her only son's efforts.

His earliest drawings of potato faces with arms and legs, over time became highly detailed replications of superhero comic book art. He remembered asking Father Smitty if priests could draw comic books. When Father laughed and said, 'You, my young friend, are God's gift. When you demonstrate the talent He blessed you with, you honor Him,' Frank felt warm and good.

For decades Frank shoved thoughts of Father Smitty as far back in his mind as he hid his comic books in the closet. He needed to drag those thoughts out of the closet, too, deal with them, and let them go.

Maria dropped Ma's scapular cross and looked his way with a guilty glance. How he missed being part of a family. This will all be OK, he told himself. I'll be OK.

Frank set aside the envelope marked *Maria*. She should go through it first. The next envelope held official papers — birth certificates, baptismal certificates, his confirmation certificate folded around a photo of Archbishop Krol, his parents' marriage certificate, and their death certificates. On a whim, Frank unfolded his parents' stiff marriage certificate. Pops and Ma were married at Saint Vincent's on November 14, 1964. Something about the date seemed off. He unfolded his own birth certificate, as dumb as that was. He knew his goddamned birth date. Still, he scanned the information. Francis Joseph Dominico, born April 5, 1965. Father: Joseph Louis Dominico. Mother: Magdalena Maria Martelli.

"Hey, Maria, get a load of this," Frank called, counting on fingers backwards from April.

Maria's breath smelled like olive oil as she leaned over him to read the marriage certificate. Her hand felt warm on his shoulder. "I don't get what's the big deal."

"Ma and Pops had to get married. They got married in November, and I was born the following April, can you believe it? Ma was three or four months pregnant with me on their wedding day."

Maria held a hand in front of her mouth. "No wonder she made me dress like a nun and be in by eleven on weekends."

"Holy Mother of God," Frank said.

"Unholy mother of Frank."

With eyebrows raised and a wide smile, Maria laughed, and Frank joined her. It felt good to laugh.

"This is great, the stuff they kept. It means a lot," he said.

Under the envelopes, he found a baseball, dingy and marked up. Happy tears filled his eyes. He wiped his nose with his sleeve. The summer he was twelve, the Springfield Cubs won the championship on his seventh-inning home run. After the game, Ma waited outside the bullpen, blocking the exit until each kid on the team signed Frank's home-run ball. He'd forgotten all about it. Now he tossed the ball up and down, imagining showing it to Rosie and the girls when he told them about his hometown. He thought they'd like Philadelphia.

As Frank rearranged the envelopes in the laundry basket, he noticed a small red envelope with a heart sticker on front. *Ma* was written in Maria's childish scrawl. She'd drawn a rainbow and a smiley face next to the heart.

"Hey, look at this card you gave Ma," Frank called.

"You look at it." A smudge ran across Maria's nose. "I need a glass of water, then I have to get home for the girls. You want anything?"

"I'm good," Frank said.

I am good, he thought. Today turned out okay. He had stuff to deal with, goddamned big stuff, but somehow, coming home, being with Maria, he was ready to deal with it. He was okay.

Instead of the Valentine's Day card Frank expected, the red envelope held a piece of stationery. When he unfolded the paper, it tore at the creases. He knit his brow. A letter from Pops to Ma?

7 September 1964

   Magdalena, the child growing within you is punishment for our sins. After you told me of your condition, I fell on my knees before Father Anthony and confessed my broken vow of chastity. As absolution, I will never lay eyes on you again. In one hour I board a train to a parish far from here where I vow to withstand temptation and serve my flock with zealous devotion.

   You have to marry Joe. He loves you. Do what you must to make him believe the child is his. Raise our child to serve the Lord as penance for our sins.

   In the love of our forgiving Savior,
   Francis.

Frank's eyes grew large, his throat tightened. He collapsed on the floor, right hand raised, fingers splayed.

"Maria," he gasped. "Maria."

Like the night he tripped the IED, a veil dropped over his eyes, and his head exploded. He understood everything now — his mother grooming him for the priesthood, her crazed obsession with saints and sacrifice, her fury when Pops told her Frankie would never be a priest.

Maria's voice rose from the stairwell. "Frankie, you coming or what? Frankie?"

The stairs creaked as her footsteps came close. Before Maria came through the door, he got to his feet, and stared out the window, his body shielding the terrible letter.

"Frankie?" Maria said, voice soft, like Ma's.

He opened the window, tore up the letter, and watched the pieces scatter in the breeze.

"Ma wanted to love me," he said. "But when she looked at me, she saw her sin."

Marie's eyes filled with alarm. "You're making no sense, Frankie."

"Go ahead, Maria, go home to your family." Frank took a deep breath. "I got some things to do here. Does the dinner invite stand?"

"You're my brother, Frankie. What do you think?" She backed out of the room. "You really okay?"

Frank listened for the front door to close. He took a breath and closed his eyes, steeling his mind like before combat. He unhooked Ma's cane from the headboard, tapped his shoe, swaggered to Ma's bureau, and set his feet in a batter's stance. He took a few practice swings.

And then, he swung through, smashing every statue on Ma's dresser. He tossed up votive candles, and slammed them as they fell. His heart beat with power, his brain focused like on the battlefield.

In elegant fury, Frank walked down the hall. Sweat dripped through his hair and trickled down his face. He tossed the cane from hand to hand as he entered his bedroom.

"Francis," he told the statue through gritted teeth, "you destroyed my mother." He yanked Saint Francis off the stand and, with a superhero burst of strength, hurled it against the cast iron radiator. "Repair yourself."

In Maria's bedroom, Saint Anthony, hands raised in blessing, teetered on his shelf.

"Saint Anthony, Saint Anthony, please come around. Something is lost and can't be found."

Frank whacked the shelf until the statue plummeted toward the floor. He shattered it in midair.

Rage consumed him like it had each time his platoon confronted enemy combatants. He didn't remember taking the stairs to the main floor, but shards of thirty-seven statues lay scattered across the living room floor. Frank scanned the room, ready to fight, oblivious to tiny cuts on his face and hands.

He brushed plaster off a chair and sat with the cane across his knees, exhausted.

HE'D MADE A GODDAMNED mess of the place, but tomorrow he'd clean it up. Don't come, he'd tell Maria. You've done enough. Now it's my turn. He made a mental list of the tools and supplies he needed. He'd repair the house for himself, for Rosie, and the twins.

In the kitchen, Frank rinsed his hands in the sink and ran the washrag over his face. After he cleaned up, he'd buy flowers for Maria, a six-pack for Mike, and ice cream for Teresa and Lucy. He'd give Rosie a call, and tell her she's been on his mind. Next week he'll stop by and make them a Philly dinner — spaghetti with tomato gravy.

He checked his watch. Enough time to change at the hotel and get to the store before dinner at Maria's.

As he started for the front door, he felt someone watching. On the landing, as if waiting her turn, plaster Maria Goretti studied him. Frank returned the faultless statue's gaze.

"*Peace be with you,*" he imagined Maria Goretti saying.

"*And also with you,*" he said. "Amen."

4

THE WITCH

A lifetime passes in the blink of an eye. The old ways become curiosities, objects to regard and reject. A lifetime ago, I lived with my parents and brothers in an old house on an old street on the outskirts of Philadelphia. For generations, descendants of Daniel Falkner, who followed Kelpius to the caves above the Wissahickon Creek, have lived in the small mill town seven miles upstream from Mystics Cave.

EACH TIME I rode my bike through town, someone greeted me with, 'You're a Falkner. It's all over your face.' At those words, my cheeks flamed, and I traced the thin white scar on my upper lip. I rarely spoke, ashamed of my lisp.

Being the schoolyard laughingstock left me anxious, and exhausted, and desperate for solitude. Most days after school, while our mother started dinner and my little brothers sat in front of the TV, I headed outside for the woods and the Wissahickon Creek. A shortcut to the creek ran through the woods alongside a small stone cottage overgrown with ivy and surrounded by brush. Kids said the elderly woman who lived in the cottage was a witch.

The day Mr. O'Kane, the mail man, told my parents he saw me entering the woods by the stone cottage, my parents forbade me to take the shortcut.

"What if something happened to you? How would we find you?" my mother asked, her face grey, and her lips pressed tight.

"The old lady in the cottage would find me," I told her, my eyes straying to the television.

My father slapped his newspaper on the coffee table and rose to his feet. "Stay away from the cottage, Betsy. That's the end of it."

Still, each time I headed for the Wissahickon, after looking over my shoulder, I took the forbidden path.

As soon as I reached the water's edge, I skipped stones, watched ripples form and fade, and wondered about the witch.

ON A WARM EVENING in September 1957, my brothers and I sat on our front porch eating salted pumpkin seeds. Henry Falkner, our doctor and my mother's cousin, had come to visit. Quiet conversation drifted through the living room window. When I heard, *Old Elizabeth's cottage,* I shimmied closer and strained to hear.

"We should come to a decision, Liz," Dr. Henry said. "The cottage is an eyesore."

"I have mixed feelings, Henry. I hate to think I'd be responsible for tearing it down," Mother said. "It's been in the family since 1748, the year the first Elizabeth was born."

"Think about it. Old Elizabeth won't live forever," Dr. Henry said.

THE NEXT AFTERNOON, while our mother bustled in the kitchen and my little brothers chased a ball in our fenced backyard, I rode my bike down the street, headed for the Wissahickon Creek. Before I entered the narrow path through the woods, I stopped to contemplate the cottage's granite cornerstone, etched with the year 1748. I envisioned a boy chiseling the granite under his master's steady gaze. If I ran my finger through the straight smooth numbers, I fancied the boy would feel my touch.

Along the path, I pushed my bike over tendrils of ivy that clutched my ankles like beggars. The dank reek of flowers in the last bloom of summer harked of ancient times when Indians crept along this very path to fish in the Wissahickon. A purple martin chortled from a pine tree high above. A wisp of smoke floated through the trees. From behind a hickory, its mottled bark rough on my cheek, I peeked towards the witch's yard.

A gaunt figure stood on a rock terrace, skirt fluttering in the breeze. Rosemary, mint, and lavender-scented smoke billowed from a fire pit in the yard where, I supposed, the witch cooked her victims. Although I hid behind the tree, when I snuck a look, her eyes locked on mine. After she stirred the ashes with a poker, she raised her hand and beckoned me. I dropped my bike and ran to the creek, afraid to look back.

My heart pounded. As I sat on the creek bank, I struggled to catch my breath. I lay back on the cool grass and gazed at the sky, where thick white clouds formed sailing ships. Soon, my hands stopped shaking. I skipped stones in the creek and watched ripples disappear in the water's flow.

As I studied the veins of a red maple leaf, I wondered what sort of girl the witch had been. Did she long for quiet and solitude? Did she cringe when her parents argued? While her mother wept, did she nestle her little brothers in her arms, begging them to be quiet? Did she run through the woods to the creek and skip stones?

TOWARD THE END OF OCTOBER, a few days before my thirteenth birthday on Halloween, a virulent illness swept my neighborhood. Now, I know it as the Asian flu pandemic of 1957, but then I knew only that my mother and brothers' cheeks burned red with fever and their eyes were glassy and frightened. My father's eyes were glassy and frightened too, although like me, he had no symptoms. Before he flew to Chicago for a conference on surviving an atom bomb attack, he called our school to report the family's illness. As he packed his bags, he bade me take care of my sick family.

Coughs and moans kept me awake, and I shook with fear my mother and brothers would die because I didn't know how to care for them. The day after my father left, Dr. Henry stopped by. I followed him from room to room and watched him shake his head when he read the thermometer. My mother and brothers' pajamas and sheets were soaked from sweat. Even though they were covered with blankets, they shivered.

I must make sure they drank water, ginger ale, something every hour, Dr. Henry told me. My mother should take Bayer aspirin and the boys, St. Joseph's. Before Dr. Henry walked out the door, he told me to place cold washcloths on their foreheads.

AFTER TWO DAYS, my mother tried to get up but collapsed. Somehow, I dragged her back to bed. The boys had stopped crying by then and lay on their beds, limp. I went from one to the other, dripping water on their lips and begging them to drink.

Early the next morning, Dr. Henry came by again. When he pressed the stethoscope against my mother's back, he knit his brows and narrowed his eyes. Before he noticed me watching from the doorway, he sighed and shook his head. He poured alcohol on a thick pad, and dabbed my mother's face, neck, and arms. Then, he cupped his hands on her cheeks and kissed her forehead.

"Please get well, Liz," Dr. Henry said.

"She's going to die, isn't she? And my brothers, too. It's my fault. I couldn't make them drink enough," I cried.

"Your mother and the boys are very ill, Betsy. There's only so much we can do," he said.

When I followed Dr. Henry downstairs, I felt broken and desperate. "I can't take care of them," I whispered.

In the doorway, he paused and stared at the pasture across the road, as if the lowing cows held the answer. I read the headline on the newspaper folded under his arm — *No Trick or Treat Tonight for Thousands Felled by Flu.* No birthday cake for me, either.

Dr. Henry touched my chin and leaned over, like he was telling me a secret. "Run down to the cottage. Ask Elizabeth to come." His face was grim.

I made a quick round of the sick rooms and left glasses of water by my mother's and brothers' beds. In the kitchen, bowls of cold soup, every glass in the house, and clumps of dried cereal littered the stove, table, countertop, and sink. Damp smelly sheets and clothing lay piled in the back kitchen.

Still in pajamas and slippers, I pulled on a tattered sweater and ran to the witch's cottage. Fear my mother and brothers would die overwhelmed my fear of the witch.

In the damp chilly dawn, I knocked quietly, hoping the witch would be asleep. Shivers rattled my body, and I wanted to lie down on the doorstep and sleep, but images of my mother, hair wet and matted across her forehead, my three-year-old brother limp in his crib, the seven-year-old twins, flailing and coughing, stirred my fist and I pounded the door, crying, "Miz Lithbeth, Miz Lithbeth!"

"Betsy James, come in. I've been waiting for you. Don't worry, Child, I've known great sickness before," the witch said, leaning on her cane. A thin white scar ran down her upper lip.

Inside, the house smelled of old books and dried fruit. Lace doilies covered the arms of a gold-striped sofa and matching chair. A black pot dangled in a stone fireplace. While the witch chose packets from a roll-top desk and dropped them in her leather bag, the furniture stared at me. From the backs of the sofa and chair, carved eagles with piercing eyes looked ready to pounce. Clawed feet flared from furniture legs and rose to winged arms.

When I sat on the sofa, the room filled with people, their sweat mingling with the smell of meat stew and beer. Their cheerful voices welcomed me. When the witch draped a mustard-colored shawl across my shoulders, I felt at home.

"Come, Betsy James, there's no time to spare," Miss Elizabeth said.

As we left the house, the witch, tall and thin, swung a forest-green cape over her woolen dress. Her thick-heeled black shoes crunched through the fallen leaves, and I had to run to keep up, even though she leaned heavy on her cane. The head of the cane was a dragon. Its glowing red eyes stared straight ahead as if guarding the clear crystal ball clenched in its teeth. Carved scales covered the shaft like a totem pole. I longed to hold the cane, and run my fingers over its scales.

After we crossed the front porch and entered our house, Miss Elizabeth hurried upstairs to tend my ailing family. Almost paralyzed by fatigue and hunger, I staggered into the living room and fell to my hands and knees. On the arm of a ladder-back chair, the witch had rested her cane. I reached for it.

The handle was rubbed smooth on top but the dragon's ruby eyes sparkled above flared nostrils. When I held the cane one way, the dragon leered like a wolf ready to strike, but when I turned it, the dragon seemed wise and kind. As I rubbed the cane between my hands, I forgot my sick family, my dirty house, my empty stomach, and my absent father. I lost myself in the dragon.

"BETSY JAMES," the witch said, leaning over me.

I jumped to my feet. I had fallen asleep on the floor, clutching the dragon cane.

"I didn't hurt it," I said and returned her cane.

"Come here," she said. She patted the threadbare sofa.

Miss Elizabeth smelled fresh, of lavender and mint, pine and parsley. I sat close and breathed it in.

"Sometimes, Child, the ancient cures work better than penicillin and other medicines my nephew and modern doctors like to use. The Falkners have studied the healing arts for as long as there have been Falkners in the world."

"Are you a witch? Are you two hundred years old?" I asked. My mortal fear had disappeared.

"I think you must be hungry, Betsy James," was all she said.

The house smelled as fresh as the woods. In the kitchen, a bowl of mushroom soup was set at my place with a slice of dark bread and a cup of tea, sweet and fragrant, different from the black tea my mother brewed. Dishes were neatly stacked in the drainer, the stovetop and counters were clear, the spills and spatters were gone. In the back kitchen, the washing machine swished, and outside, white sheets flapped under a cold sun.

Miss Elizabeth sat across from me at the kitchen table. She handed me a small burlap bag fastened with a drawstring. The bag smelled of strawberries, peppermint, and ginger.

"In an hour, brew this tea for your mother and brothers, not too hot for the boys, and give them another cup in the evening. They'll be much better tomorrow," she said.

Then the witch took my hand, opened my fingers and dropped three tiny eggs in my palm.

"These are for you, an All Hallows Eve treat. Let them melt in your mouth. I'll let myself out."

After the witch swung her cape over her shoulders, clutched her leather bag to her chest, opened the door, and left us, I ran upstairs to check my mother and brothers. All of them slept, their breaths soft, their foreheads cool.

When I returned to the kitchen, I found the dragon cane swinging on the back of a kitchen chair. I picked it up and ran out the door.

"You forgot the cane," I called, waving it like a flag.

But she was gone. Not a sign of her down the road. I smiled when I realized I'd have to visit Miss Elizabeth to return her cane.

After I set my dishes in the sink, I popped the egg-shaped candy in my mouth. They were sweet but not like sugar, not like fruit – a creamy sweet, soft and slippery, smooth and warm. The candy clicked against my teeth as I trudged upstairs, tears streaming down my cheeks, weight lifting off my shoulders like steam from a pot.

In her bedroom, my mother leaned against a pillow, wan but alert. The room smelled like strawberries and peppermint.

"How are the boys?" she whispered, "and how are you?"

Sounds of giggling came from the twins' room and a moment later, they carried in little Tommy, the three of them skinny but clean and happy. When they climbed into bed with my mother, I did too, inhaling the bleachy smell of clean sheets.

By the time my father returned, all of us felt fine.

SNOW AND COLD came early that year and the ground stayed snow covered into spring. No one went out much, frightened of the Asian flu.

On a sunny Saturday in March, after the weather warmed and the days grew long, I walked down the road to visit Miss Elizabeth and return the cane that hung on my bedpost all those months since she helped us.

The old stone cottage looked dilapidated, decrepit, deserted. I rapped the front door with the cane.

Mr. O'Kane, the mailman, saw me, and stopped his truck. "Betsy James, what are you doing? No one lives in the old Falkner place."

"Where's Miss Elizabeth? Where did she go?" I asked, my throat so tight I could hardly speak.

"The flu took her away," Mr. O'Kane said, "the terrible flu."

Outside the cottage, I sat on a crumbling step and ran my finger through the numbers on the cornerstone, envisioning long cold winters, squash soup bubbling in a black pot, and a tall thin girl sitting by the Wissahickon Creek, skipping stones.

A LIFETIME AGO, my brothers moved away, reluctant to return even to stand by me at our mother and father's funerals. The old house we lived in no longer exists, replaced by a row of luxury townhouses. Across the road, parents in lawn chairs watch children kick balls on a cow pasture now covered with plastic grass.

And I with my old ways have become a curiosity to regard and reject. Yet, when I lean on my cane and make my way through the woods alongside my cottage, I feel the earth under my feet.

On the bank of Wissahickon Creek, I skip stones, watch ripples, and wait for a girl with a scar on her lip to knock on my door and come in.

ORIGINALLY PUBLISHED by *Rose Red Review,* Issue No. 6, Autumn 2013.

5

ROLL ON

Four days after her husband of forty-three years died, Althea Taylor stared at shelves of sugar, flour, baking soda, and cake mixes. Now that she was here, she couldn't remember why she roused herself off the recliner and drove to the Acme supermarket. She leaned on her cart's handle, too weary to move. The bag of sweet potatoes in her cart jogged her memory. She came for ingredients for Henry's favorite sweet potato pie to serve tomorrow at the gathering after his funeral. While she searched for evaporated milk, Althea heard singing from the next aisle.

Over hill, over dale, we will hit the dusty trail . . .

Althea sang back, *And the caissons go rolling along . . .*

She dropped four cans of evaporated milk in her cart and a jar of organic ginger. When she swung around to move to the check out line, she nearly collided with a trollish-looking fellow who marched with his cart in time to the Army anthem. He jerked to a halt and stared, without making eye contact.

"You know my song," he said, his voice surprisingly resonant.

"My father was a soldier," Althea said, surprised at herself for engaging in conversation with the odd person.

They contemplated each other for a long time. Althea took in his dark blue pants and Dickies shirt with a public schools patch on the pocket. A ring of keys hung from his cracked black belt. His fingers were short and stubby, with filthy fingernails. Thick eyebrows the rusty color of his hair bulged over wide-set brown eyes, but his face was without expression. Althea stared at his large pointy ears.

"I never met a black person who knows *The Caisson Song*," the strange man said.

"Black people know lots of things," Althea answered, annoyed. The fairy tale about three billy goats Gruff and the troll came to mind. She didn't care to cross a bridge over this troll's house.

"People like me know lots of things, too." He stared at her feet.

Outside the front plate glass windows the October sky grew dark.

"It's getting late. I must be going." Althea's heart pounded and she felt a headache coming on — her blood pressure was rising.

"You know the ghost by the door?" the man asked.

"The Halloween ghost?" Why did she engage in this conversation?

"He's not alive. When the door opens he says, *Happy Halloween, I'm a friendly ghost,* but he's not alive."

"I won't talk to him, then." How odd, she thought.

As she hurried down the aisle to the checkout line, the singer's voice followed — *Then it's Hi! Hi! Hee! in the field artillery, shout out your numbers loud and strong . . .*

For the first time since she found Henry at the bottom of the stairs, brown skin dusky and eyes fixed, Althea focused on something other than grief. *Over hill, over dale* looped through her brain.

THE LAST GROUP of mourners finally left Althea's house as the sky grew dim. Now only her three daughters – Henrietta, Deondra, and Tamara remained. Henry named their oldest daughter for himself and their favorite singer, Etta James. Henrietta never liked the name. Even as an attorney, she went by Hettie.

While Althea closed her eyes, Deondra and Tamara washed dishes and wrapped leftovers. The house smelled of lemon furniture polish, vanilla-scented candles, and Henry's favorite sweet potato pie. Henry's scent, earthy and warm, was locked in their bedroom closet.

From the second floor, Hettie's footsteps creaked over hardwood and thudded over rugs. What is that child doing? Althea wondered, but she was too exhausted, her brain too numb for more than a passing thought. The pills her doctor prescribed got her through this terrible week but left her mouth dry and her brain foggy. No more Xanax. She needed to think her way through the upcoming months and years. She needed to plan for life without Henry. His sudden death was a shock.

Althea pressed the side button and her recliner moved upright. Near the fireplace, the magazine basket brimmed with the travel brochures Henry collected. After he retired two years ago, he begged Althea to put in her retirement papers. 'Now it's our time,' he said, 'to take those trips we always dreamed of.'

Somewhat reluctantly since she loved her position in the elementary school office, Althea joined Henry in retirement. Now she was grateful. They'd taken three cruises – to Alaska, the Caribbean, and Greece. They drove west and spent a week at a dude ranch in Wyoming. They took the grandchildren to Disney World. Three months ago, they spent a week in Gettysburg with Hettie, babysitting when the nanny went on vacation.

Althea wished her daughters would leave so she could rest.

"Moms." Hettie touched Althea's shoulder. "Are you awake?"

Althea opened her eyes, surprised she'd fallen asleep. She took Hettie's hand and held it, as if to gain strength. Deondra and Tamara, less than a year apart, and raised like twins, sat on the loveseat, resting their chins on their palms. Their deep brown eyes were sad and concerned. Althea smiled and released Hettie's hand.

"Your father was so proud of you girls. I'll miss him dearly."

Eyes filled with tears, Tamara bounced off the loveseat and knelt beside her. Althea noticed Hettie brought down the box of financial documents.

"Daddy's death came as a shock to all of us," Hettie said. "We know how hard this is for you, and how much harder it's going to get. But we love you, and we'll help you. I'll take care of the legalities –

probate, death notices, contacting the life insurance company, transferring assets, all of that."

"Thank you, Hettie. I'm not of a mind to deal with the paperwork," Althea said.

Deondra from the loveseat and Tamara beside her, expressions wary, glanced at Hettie.

Deondra blurted, "You don't have to live alone, Moms."

Hettie glared at her sister then turned to Althea. "We know you haven't had time to think about the future, but we've discussed it at length. We hate to think of you alone in this old house. We want you to live with one of us."

"Moms, Alonzo and I would love you to move in with us. The boys are crazy about you and we have plenty of room. You would feel right at home since we live so close," Deondra said.

Tamara lifted her sweet eyes. "You could live with us in West Chester. You could even sit in on classes Jerome and I teach at the college. Why don't you come for a long visit when you're up to it? We can shop downtown and have lunch in one of the new restaurants."

"And you know we'd love you to come to Gettysburg. I miss having my mother close," Hettie said.

"You girls are my blessing, but I'm perfectly capable of living alone. This is my home. I belong right here." Althea sighed and turned her eyes to Hettie, then Deondra, then Tamara. "I'm only sixty-four. I could live another twenty years, even more." She hesitated then said, "I might go back to work."

I might go back to work. Her own words surprised her. As soon as she said them out loud, a weight dropped off her shoulders. The girls' stares burned into her heart.

"You worked your whole life, Moms, even when we were growing up. Daddy would want you to relax, enjoy your grandchildren, take trips to all those places you dreamed of," Tamara said.

Hettie knit her eyebrows in the scowl Althea knew terrified opposing attorneys. Deondra rocked in her seat. Tamara trembled.

"I loved your father since I was a teenager. I can't imagine life without him, but traveling was his dream. My dream is to stay put where I belong. My dream is to keep busy with work I enjoy. The only way I know I'll get up each morning and go out that door is if I have a job." Althea closed her eyes a moment. "I put my future in God's hands. *Fear not, for I am with you. Be not dismayed, for I am your God. I will strengthen you. I will help you. I will uphold you with my righteous hand.*" She felt stirrings of hunger she'd ignored while seeing to her guests. "Now please don't talk about this anymore, and tell me there's a bite left of sweet potato pie."

An hour later, after insisting she truly wanted some time alone, Althea watched the girls climb into Deondra's silver minivan and disappear into darkness. Restless, she roamed the first floor. She opened the refrigerator, and took out the pie, a slice of ham, and a pickle. Before she settled into her recliner, she put an Etta James CD in the stereo. She needed the music she and Henry loved.

When their song came on, Althea sang along — *You got to roll with me, Henry . . . roll on, roll on, roll on* — swaying as if she were dancing. And then she cried.

THE NEXT MORNING before her daughters and death business — death certificates, life insurance policies, transfers of ownership, IRAs, and Henry's clothing, books, tools, and golf clubs – overwhelmed her, Althea made coffee and turned on her laptop. She searched for job openings in nearby elementary school offices. Nothing. She scrolled past listings for school nurses and groundskeepers. A position at McCleary Bunch Washington, the high school her girls had attended, drew her interest – Compliance Coordinator, Activities and Athletics Office. Before she attached her resume to the online application, she checked the driveway for Deondra's minivan. Not here yet. She read over her application. As soon as she heard the crunch of wheels and a car door slam, she pressed submit and shut down her laptop. She put an *Oprah* magazine on top of it and shoved it aside.

The front door opened and Hettie called, "Moms?"

"I'm here," she answered and met her three girls in the foyer. Her eyes shifted as if she'd done something nefarious.

"Are you OK?" Tamara took Althea's trembling hand.

"I'll be fine," Althea said. She should have deleted the history on her laptop. She'd do that as soon as the girls left.

HER DAUGHTERS WERE RIGHT ABOUT one thing – being alone unnerved her, especially at night. Without Henry's snores, branches tapping against glass transformed into thieves breaking windows, creaks became burglars testing locks, rain on the roof turned into bats in the attic. Althea slept with a flashlight, a broomstick, and her cell phone at her side. Silly, she knew. As soon as she got herself out and about instead of spending her days missing Henry and feeling sorry for herself, she'd feel better about everything.

The first week of November – three weeks after Henry's funeral – Althea sipped coffee as she skimmed the Target weekly ad. She scolded herself for coming downstairs before she showered and dressed. She searched a drawer for a pen and wrote a shopping list on the back of an envelope. The phone rang.

"Good morning. This is Sharon Murphy from M. B. Washington High School. We have your application for the Compliance Coordinator position in the Athletics and Activities Office. Are you available for an interview tomorrow afternoon?"

Althea's mind raced. She hadn't expected to get an interview. She hadn't done this sort of work before. Should she admit to Sharon she wasn't qualified? She figured the interview would sort that out in a hurry.

"Yes, of course. What time shall I be there?"

"Three o'clock. School lets out at 2:30. Clayton – Clayton Thompson is the activities director – thought you'd be more comfortable then. Do you know how to get here?"

"Oh, yes. My daughters graduated from McCleary Bunch."

Upstairs, Althea chose an interview outfit. She called her hairdresser and made an appointment for that afternoon.

"Listen to me, Henry," she said out loud. "I need to do this. I need to try. You know I can't sit around and do nothing."

Henry's voice in her head told her, *You go, Girl!*

~

INSIDE THE SUBARU she and Henry bought a year ago, Althea sang with Etta James, *Oh, oh, sometimes, I get a good feeling.*

Later, with her curly grey hair cut tight the way she liked, and her nails shiny coral, Althea drove to Target. She needed hose for her interview. Her girls made fun whenever Althea wore stockings, but she was a grown woman, an older woman, not some skinny-legged girl in her thirties.

As she turned into the lot, her fingers gripped the steering wheel. Maybe I should call and cancel the interview, she thought. No, she decided, Althea Taylor is smart, and strong, and ready to roll. Time to *roll while the rolling is on.* She noticed a minivan pulling out of a spot near the front. How lucky, she thought, put on her blinker, waited for the minivan to exit, then slid right in. She reached for her purse and dropped her keys in a side pocket. As she approached the store entrance, a car horn blasted and brakes screeched. Althea gasped when a white Vespa motor scooter headed for a handicapped space cut off a black pickup truck.

The air smelled of gasoline and burnt rubber. When the pickup driver climbed out and slammed his door, Althea stepped behind a line of carts, clutching her purse to her chest. Her eye twitched.

The rugged-looking man with brown hair in a ponytail loomed over the Vespa driver, shouting, "What the hell's wrong with you, Retard! You're lucky I didn't run you down."

As soon as she heard, *retard*, Althea took a breath and pushed past other shoppers to stand beside the Vespa driver whose helmet and visor covered his face.

Retard, nigger, chink, spic, rag head, bitch, faggot – Althea's blood boiled when bigots resorted to jeers and insults to assert their presumed superiority. What was this country coming to when even its leaders cast aspersions far and wide?

"I saw what happened," she said, voice strong. "This boy didn't intend to cut you off. He was focused on reaching the handicapped spots. No one seems to be hurt."

A woman leaned out the pickup's passenger window. "Come on,

Donny, who cares about that dipshit? You promised to take me to lunch. Let's go. I'm hungry."

"Lucky for you this lady has your back," Donny said.

Before the pickup turned onto the exit lane, Donny rolled down the window and stuck out his arm with the middle finger extended. Diesel odor lingered like an insult.

Althea bit her lower lip, wondering what became of common courtesy.

"I'm not a retard," the Vespa driver said.

"Of course you're not. That man was rude and unkind."

"I'm mainstream," he said.

Althea recognized the voice, but couldn't place it until he took off his helmet. She froze. *The Caisson Song* man from the Acme. Passersby circled away from them.

"I know you. You like my song. Are you going to Target?"

Althea cleared her throat. "Yes, and I'm in a hurry. Take care. Check both ways before you cross the parking lot."

As she headed to the store, she sensed him following. She hastened her step, grabbed a basket, and with tennis shoes squeaking over the linoleum floor, made for the hosiery section. How random, she thought, to run into that peculiar person again. The parking lot confrontation unnerved her, and shattered her plan to take her time, walk around, look at makeup, maybe buy new dishtowels. Instead, shaky, but proud she had the courage to prevent an ugly situation, Althea chose four packages of stockings.

From a few aisles over came – *Shout out your numbers loud and strong, For wherever you go, you will always know . . .* Then it stopped. Althea winced. She knew as sure as she stood there, the fellow expected her to sing the next line. She bit her lip.

While the cashier scanned Althea's items, the young mother behind her placed diapers and rash ointment on the conveyor belt and asked, "Did you see the guy marching around the store singing army songs?"

The cashier rolled his eyes. Althea shrugged.

When she hurried to the parking lot, she fought the urge to look over her shoulder. She wanted to be safe at home with a cup of tea while she reviewed the Compliance Coordinator position description, and thought up questions about job duties. After she backed out of her parking spot and drove to the exit, she sang, *That the caissons go rolling along.* It was a relief.

ALTHEA HAD DRIVEN ALMOST HALF-WAY home when she checked the rearview mirror to see what was causing the humming noise.

"Oh no, you are not following me," she muttered under her breath.

She wondered if she should call the police, but report what? That a strange man on a Vespa scooter was driving behind her on a public road? Instead, she pushed the call button on the steering wheel and said, "Call Deondra." Moments later, her daughter answered.

"Deondra, are you home? I thought I'd stop by."

When she made the turn onto Deondra's street, the white Vespa continued down Stenton Avenue. She felt relieved and a little foolish. The man certainly hadn't threatened her in any way. She parked along the curb in front of her daughter's house.

"Moms, you got your hair done. Come inside," Deondra said.

For no reason except she didn't feel up to justifying herself, Althea decided not to tell Deondra about her encounter at Target or her upcoming interview.

THE FOLLOWING day at quarter to three, the McCleary Bunch Washington High School parking lot bustled with teenagers hanging around cars. A group of boys and girls – the winter track team – ran past in shorts and sleeveless shirts not warm enough for the crisp air of early November. Beyond the parking lot, Althea spied helmeted boys practicing on the football field.

Despite visiting the high school for parent-teacher meetings and other events during the years her daughters attended, Althea wasn't sure which side to enter for the Athletics and Activities Office. She approached a group of black girls who leaned against a green Honda.

"Can you show me which door to enter for Mr. Thompson's office?"

The girls quieted. A slender girl with rings through her eyebrow asked, "Why?"

"I have an interview," Althea said, and smiled. She approved of young women speaking up, as long as they were respectful.

"That's good," the girl said. "You have to check in at the front office, through the blue door around front."

"Thank you."

"Good luck," six girls called.

After she checked in, Althea found the Athletic Department hallway. The scuffed linoleum floor oozed odors from fifty years of sneakered footsteps. A disheveled boy limped past and entered a door marked, Athletic Training. As Althea slowed to read names on doors, a red-haired woman stepped out of an office and waved.

"I'm Sharon. You must be Althea. We're so happy you came."

Althea smiled at the woman's bubbly tone as well as her dazzling sweater, with a regally-dressed blue-eyed lion, a dignified deer, and a noble fox decorating the front. The image brought to mind *The Chronicles of Narnia*. Althea wondered if she entered a fantasy world. She ignored the impulse to curtsy and say, Your Majesty.

The reception area of the Activities and Athletics Department was furnished with a battered metal desk, a tired black chair on rollers, and a blue plastic side chair. A narrow table flush against the back wall held a scorched coffee machine and foam cups. Colorful posters of handsome male and female athletes engaging in various sports decorated the walls. A glass-paneled door marked *Director* opened to an office on the right. Another office was on the left.

"Your office," Sharon said.

Sharon knocked on the director's door and ushered Althea inside. A strapping black man with tight white hair, a thin mustache, and kind brown eyes behind wire-rimmed spectacles rose to greet her.

"I finally have the honor of meeting the famous Althea Taylor." Clayton Thompson spoke with a distinct British accent. "When Sharon called your references, your elementary school principal insisted on speaking with me. Mr. Nash told me you've just suffered the loss of your husband. You have our deepest sympathy. I realize this is a difficult time for you, but if you're up to returning to work, Mr. Nash said I should get you on board and get out of your way. So my interview question is, can you start Monday?"

Althea's throat went dry. She clung to the manila envelope filled with work samples and letters of reference. She never expected to be offered the position before she said a word. She stared wide-eyed at the director.

"Perhaps you have a few questions before you decide?"

She took a breath and rallied. "What are my duties?"

"All of them." The director's expression remained alert.

Althea knit her brow. "Is there a dress code?"

He nodded, expression serious. "Indeed there is. Every Activities and Athletics staff member is required to dress. I tolerate no nudity."

"In that case, I accept," Althea said, not able to suppress a smile.

Sharon clapped and said, "Yay."

AFTER ALTHEA COMPLETED the paperwork for payroll, she returned to the almost empty parking lot. As she inhaled the sharp essence of asphalt, she reminded herself to calm down and walk with dignity.

In a small handicapped parking space against the building, a white Vespa scooter caught her eye. It can't be, she thought. But then she recalled her first run-in with *The Caisson Song* man. The image of the public school emblem on his pocket flooded her brain. Apprehension clouded her mind, eclipsed only by anxiety at the prospect of telling her daughters about her job. She hurried to the car. Before she slid inside, she looked over her shoulder.

On the drive home, Althea sang with Etta, *Strange things happening every day*. Then she squared her shoulders and rehearsed telling her daughters she accepted a job at the high school.

MONDAY, Althea arrived at 7:15 am, more than an hour before her contractual starting time. As she popped her car trunk to retrieve her bags, she sensed a presence behind her. Startled, she whipped around, heart racing and hands clenched. The *Caisson* man stumbled backwards into a parked car.

"What are you doing here?" she and he asked simultaneously.

"I work here," she and he answered, again simultaneously.

If she hadn't been so startled, she might have found their interchange amusing. As it was, she just wanted him to go away. A boy's voice came from across the parking lot.

"Hey, Lucky, leave that lady alone or I'll report you."

Four white boys jogged toward Althea and the little man they called Lucky, who blinked.

"You should go now," Althea said.

Lucky lowered his eyes and shuffled toward the school, muttering to himself. His gait was unusual; his toes struck before his heels in a hoppy motion.

When the boys reached her, a blond kid with a ruddy complexion and hazel eyes asked, "Was he bothering you, Ma'am? Because I'll report him if he was. He's been told to keep away from the girls. He scares them. Are you a substitute teacher?"

"Today's my first day in the Athletics and Activities Office," Althea said. "Does he work here? Is his name Lucky?"

Another boy, stocky, with acne and lank brown hair spoke up.

"He's a janitor. We call him Lucky because he looks like the leprechaun from *Lucky Charms*."

"I see," Althea said.

Overhead, a flock of small birds flew by, chittering in the cool breeze.

"I don't know why they let him work here," the third boy said.

"People say he went to school here, like ten or twenty years ago," the fourth boy added.

Althea turned back to her trunk and reached for her supplies. As she lifted the heavy bag, the first boy nudged the youngest.

"I'll carry that for you, Ma'am," the kid said.

"I appreciate that," Althea said, surprised and impressed.

WHEN SHE PUSHED OPEN the Athletics and Activities Office door, a burned coffee smell assailed her. The boy dropped her bag inside the door, and hurried down the hall. Before Althea crossed to her office, Sharon bustled in, a purple backpack slung on her shoulders and a chocolate cake in her hands. On Sharon's yellow sweatshirt an embroidered giraffe munched leaves. Her yellow sneakers matched her top.

"You beat me in even though I came extra early," Sharon said in her girlish voice. "I hope you like chocolate. I thought, wouldn't it be nice to have a cake to celebrate Althea's first day?" She set down the cake and slipped off the backpack. "Don't you look nice? You put me to shame."

"You look very bright," Althea said, and smoothed her silk blouse.

While Sharon poured fresh water in the coffee maker, Althea stepped beside her.

"When does Mr. Thompson get in?"

"Clayton normally gets in around nine, sometimes ten, because he stays late most nights for games, plays, concerts, whatever the kids are up to. That works for me because it gives me an hour to tidy up his office. He leaves everything in piles. I don't know how he finds anything. We're both happy you agreed to work with us. We need you to organize and update the kids' records." Sharon lowered her eyes and blushed. "The truth is, Althea, we've misplaced some kids' emergency information and medical permission slips. We've been lucky so far, but if the main office ever did an audit, we'd be in deep doggy do."

"Then I better start coordinating compliance."

Before Althea had a chance to ask Sharon to explain the filing system, a shushing sound came from the hallway, then stopped. Sharon appeared unperturbed, but Althea felt nervous, as if she were skating on thin ice, waiting for the surface to crack. And then it did.

Over hill, over dale, we will hit the dusty trail . . . then that pause, that hanging line begging for completion. After a few seconds, the broom began shushing, and the song moved down the hall. *And the caissons go*

rolling along. In and out, hear them shout, counter march and right about,
and the caissons go rolling along.

After the words faded away, Althea peeked out the door. Except for
a few teenagers wearing guilty expressions, the hallway was empty.
When she turned, Sharon was right behind her.

"That was Lucky, the janitor," Sharon said.

"I met him in the parking lot."

Sharon didn't need to hear about Althea's encounters at the grocery
store and Target. Instead, Althea telepathically begged Sharon to tell
her about Lucky.

"He's not right," Sharon said. "Clayton says he has social and
cognitive issues. He has physical problems, too. I'm not sure what they
are, but doesn't he look like a leprechaun? That's why everyone calls
him Lucky."

Althea swallowed. "Is he dangerous?"

Sharon shrugged. "Not really. He's done some inappropriate things
by mistake. Last semester he went into the girls' locker room and stood
gaping. He would have been fired, but one of the boys confessed he
told Lucky the coach wanted him to collect the towels right away."

Althea wrinkled her nose. "That was mean."

Sharon let out a breath. She tapped her fingers on her desktop,
raised her eyes to the ceiling then let out a sigh. "I guess you'll find out
eventually. We had a first year athletic trainer quit because she said
Lucky made her nervous. I don't know. He doesn't bother me."

Althea wondered if the young athletic trainer knew the words to
The Caisson Song.

NIGHTS after she checked the locks, dimmed the lights, and got in bed,
Althea tossed and turned. Every creak, every tap, even the shudder
when the furnace turned on brought to mind images of dark-clothed
burglars creeping around her house. This was a good, safe
neighborhood, but whenever a late night siren wailed, Althea sat bolt
upright, heart pounding. Some nights, as she lay awake, she told
Henry she was angry with him for dying.

But with her new job, each morning she woke confident and ready
to go. She found comfort in the routine of dressing, drinking coffee,
and reading the paper before heading out the door at seven. Work took
her mind off losing Henry. She often thought of the years they worked
together to instill in their daughters the values of education, hard
work, and self respect. Much of their earnings went to the girls' college
tuitions, including graduate school for Deondra and Tamara, and law
school for Hettie. We did a fine job, she told Henry. Our daughters are
intelligent, competent, and beautiful women. She wished she could tell
him in person.

Now, work was Althea's salvation, the place where grief stepped
aside for a few hours. After her daughters realized how much Althea
enjoyed work, even Hettie agreed she made the right decision.

ON A BLUSTERY NOVEMBER AFTERNOON, Althea was in her office when
Clayton called, "Sharon, I need you to deliver Jimmy Smith's jock strap
to the wrestling office."

Althea poked her head in Clayton's office. "Sharon had to pick up a
prescription at Walgreens. Is there something I can help with?"

Clayton held out a small nylon bag. "Jimmy Smith forgot his
wrestling gear. His mother dropped it off." He pushed back his chair
and rose. "No worries, I'll give it to the coach. We don't want little
Jimmy to miss practice."

"I'll do it," Althea said, "as long as I don't have to actually touch
the jock strap."

As she walked down the hall, Althea held the bag at arms length.
She recognized the wrestling gym by its wolf den smell, and the
trophy case filled with gold-plated boys locked together in
disconcerting positions. The most distressing trophy was a metallic
boy on his hands while another tin boy upended his legs. She shook
her head and muttered, "I don't see the glory in brutality."

As she turned away, intent on finding the wrestling coach's office
and delivering Jimmy Smith's whatever, from around the corner keys
rattled, and a broom shushed.

She'd only taken a few steps when *Over hill, over dale, as we hit the dusty trail . . .* drew close. There was no escape. A lifetime of good manners prevented her from hurrying away. In the moment she hesitated, Lucky's tiptoed gait brought him beside her. He smelled of dirt and ammonia. His eyes flitted back and forth, but his pasty face remained expressionless.

"Why don't you like my song anymore?"

Althea prayed for a coach or kid to come out of the gym. "I don't want to disturb the students."

Perspiration from her hands dampened Jimmy Smith's nylon bag. She glanced down the hallway. Her eyes settled on the trophy case.

"Those are wrestling trophies," Lucky said.

"I have something for the wrestling coach," Althea said, voice tight.

"The wrestling team won state championships in 1981, 1992, 2003, and 2014. That means they won't win again until 2025," Lucky said.

Althea wanted to ask how he knew that, but decided the less said the better. "I must get going." She took a step away.

"They didn't win the state wrestling championship when I went here – 1996, 1997, 1998, 1999. But the year I started work, 2003, they won the state championship."

Althea couldn't fathom how he knew all those dates. "Were you on the wrestling team?"

"My bones don't wrestle but I came to school, and I got my diploma. I'm mainstream."

"I have to deliver this to the coach now, Lucky."

Althea hurried down the hall to the coach's office, and slipped inside. "Clayton sent me with this bag for Jimmy Smith."

As he accepted the bag, the coach looked past her. Lucky watched, framed in the doorway. "Get back to work, Son," the coach said. He raised one eyebrow. "He never misses work. He has a routine and does OK as long as nothing disrupts it. We try to keep it that way. Do you want someone to walk you back?"

"No thanks," Althea said, but wished someone would.

∿

THANKSGIVING WEEK, a turkey in a pilgrim hat and buckle shoes smiled from Sharon's beige sweatshirt. Since Clayton flew to England to visit his elderly father, Althea planned to devote her time to organizing his office and rationalizing the file system.

Clayton was great with the kids, and the Booster Club parents found him entertaining, but he struggled to keep up with the paperwork. The daily drama of unhappy parents who demanded more playing time for their kids, students whose grades excluded them from competition, and coaches who valued sports over academics required most of his time and energy. And he misplaced everything. No document was safe once it entered his office.

Monday, Althea tackled Clayton's desk. First she sorted his inbox and identified priority issues, upcoming issues, dead issues, and for information only. She discovered a slew of documents in piles on the floor, including an enormous number of duplicates.

While Althea worked, Sharon chatted from the doorway about the Christmas decorations she planned to display. When Sharon asked if she could help, Althea suggested she shred the duplicates and outdated forms. The shredder's growl sounded like success.

By afternoon, Althea started on the file cabinets. Sharon scrounged up new hanging files and manila folders. While Althea designed a logical filing system, Sharon typed labels.

After the late bell rang, Sharon said, "I can't believe how much we got done. I don't think I've ever worked so hard."

Black streaks stained Althea's khaki slacks, and dirt ringed the cuffs of her yellow blouse. A smudge ran across her forehead. Floating dust motes made her sneeze.

"Wait until tomorrow. We'll start on the emergency medical forms," Althea said.

That night, Althea fell into an untroubled sleep.

THE NEXT MORNING, as soon as she arrived at work she ran vinegar through the coffee maker while she scoured the coffee pot in the Ladies Room. In the hallway, kids were asking, "What's that horrible smell?"

After she dumped the hot vinegar and ran clear water through a cycle, Althea doubled the filter and added scoops from a fresh bag of dark roast. While the coffee brewed, she inhaled and thought, that's how coffee should smell.

When Sharon walked through the door, Althea met her with a new porcelain mug embossed with the letter S, and filled with fresh coffee, sugar, and milk.

"What's the occasion? Oh, this is wonderful," Sharon said.

"As long as we're cleaning Clayton's mess, I figured we may as well clean the coffee maker, too," Althea said.

They clinked their mugs.

Dressed in casual blue slacks and a jersey shirt, Althea pulled student emergency forms from the files while Sharon checked they were up to date. They discovered as many forms for students who graduated as for current students.

Althea sorted the old forms alphabetically by year of graduation, and Sharon placed them in archive boxes. Current students' names went on new color-coded folders, cross-referenced by sport and activity, with a checklist for required forms by date.

By early afternoon, Althea's back and neck ached, but the files were organized. While Sharon slid the alphabetized files into drawers, Althea called the Information Technology Department.

Two girls from the advanced software class agreed to develop an Athletics and Activities database for their community service project. They assured Althea it was a piece of cake and would be ready for input before winter break.

Before then, Althea planned to follow up with each coach and each activity to check athletic and activity records against rosters to make sure McCleary Bunch Washington High School students complied with all state requirements.

Wednesday, the day before Thanksgiving, Althea brought Sharon a fresh baked sweet potato pie.

"You can't celebrate Thanksgiving without it," she said.

Sharon swooned over the sweet cinnamon smell. "This is the nicest gift ever. I doubt my family will wait until tomorrow to get into it."

When they left that afternoon, Althea and Sharon congratulated each other.

"I can't believe we got through all those documents," Sharon said. "And it's all thanks to you. Clayton should visit his Dad in England more often."

Althea squeezed Sharon's hand. "We make a good team."

When she crossed the parking lot, Althea noticed Lucky, helmet on, straddling his Vespa scooter. She thought he looked abandoned. The dark goggles turned her way. She gave a tiny nod and hurried on.

THANKSGIVING MORNING, Althea leaned into the mirror to apply magenta lipstick. She wondered if Henry would feel let down because she didn't insist on making the family dinner. But without Henry to carve the turkey and cheer for the Eagles, Althea didn't think she could bear it. When Tamara invited everyone to West Chester for the day, she felt a huge wave of relief. Today she planned to put up her feet like a queen and enjoy the grandchildren.

"Moms?" Deondra's voice carried up the steps. "Alonzo took the boys in the other car. He said you deserved to ride in peace."

After they passed through the toll booth to enter the Pennsylvania Turnpike, Deondra asked, "How's the new job?"

"I feel like I'm accomplishing something important. Clayton is a great boss, but good Lord, his office was an absolute disaster – papers in piles on the floor, files in disarray. No wonder he couldn't find anything. Since he was away this week, Sharon and I organized his files. Next month we're moving to computer-based record-keeping."

"Sharon's the secretary, right?" Deondra asked.

"Office manager. She may not be the most efficient person I ever met, but she's funny and kind, a pure spirit. She'd give you the sweatshirt off her back. And what a collection of sweaters and sweatshirts! I can't wait to see her Christmas collection. I truly enjoy listening to her chatter. It feels like forever since I laughed so much."

"And how are you managing in the house without Dad?"

"As long as I'm busy, I'm fine. That's why this job is such a blessing. To be honest, when I'm home, I have the sense I've forgotten something but can't bring it to mind. I miss your father most at night. I'll hear a creak and think he's coming up the stairs. Or I'll remember something funny Sharon said and turn to tell him. Most times I tell him anyway. I buy too many groceries and forget to put the trash out on Wednesday mornings. Still, I get by."

"Have you thought about moving in with us?" Deondra asked, voice rich with kindness.

"Please, Deondra, after all these years, I belong in that house. Now, let me enjoy the day without any talk about leaving my home."

The Monday after Thanksgiving, Althea and Sharon shared happy glances, anxious for Clayton's arrival. The clock's hands showed five minutes to nine when his footsteps approached.

With a shopping bag in each hand, he entered with a robust, "Good morning." One bag displayed the Union Jack. A red double-decker bus drove across the other. "How are my favorite ladies?"

Clayton gave them the largest Cadbury chocolate bars ever seen this side of the Atlantic, or so Althea thought. Net weight one kilogram – over two pounds of chocolate. While Althea and Sharon admired the candy, Clayton walked into his office.

A moment later, he yelled, "Who the bloody hell rearranged my office!" He returned to the reception area with a frown he struggled to maintain. "What have the likes of you been up to in my absence? The room looks absolutely livable. I'm sure I won't be able to find a bloody thing. But then, I couldn't find a bloody thing anyway, so no harm, no foul." He cracked a smile.

"Althea did it and I helped," Sharon said in her chirpiest voice.

"Well, Althea, you've sealed your fate, my dear. You may never leave us. You hold the key to the location of every important document in this office. I may invite our most honorable vice principal to visit this week. No doubt he'll experience immense agony at the sight of an organized Clayton Thompson. Yes, that's a brilliant plan. Come in, Althea. You too, Sharon, and show me where you hid my papers."

After Althea explained the filing system, all three returned to the reception area.

"And before winter break, two senior girls in the IT program promise to build a database system for our records," Sharon said.

When Sharon's eyes strayed to the door, her pleased expression turned wary. Althea and Clayton followed Sharon's gaze to the pale face pressed against the door window. Althea inched out of sight. Her stomach churned.

"Move along, Lucky," Clayton said, voice quiet, expression kind.

When the face disappeared, Althea let out a sigh. "He makes me uncomfortable."

"He gives me the heebie-jeebies," Sharon said.

"Lucky follows directions and does his work, but he's oblivious to social cues, and tends to come across as off-putting," Clayton said.

"He's not off-putting, he's mainstream," Althea said.

Clayton, eyebrows raised, looked at her with curiosity. "You've been talking to the lad."

"The lad's been talking to me. A few weeks before I started work, not long after Henry died, while I was shopping at Acme someone sang the first line of *The Caisson Song*." Althea lowered her eyes. "Without thinking I sang the next line. He came into my aisle looking for me. Now he seems to seek me out. It's unsettling. When he corners me, I'm uncomfortable, but it feels rude to walk away."

"I wonder what goes on in his head. Do you know you can tell him your birth date, and he can tell you what day of the week it falls on? Yet we have to remind him he's not permitted to approach the girls. I don't think he realizes he's a grown man," Clayton said.

"How long has he worked here?" Althea asked.

Clayton sighed. "Since 2002. Years ago, including when Lucky attended high school here, his mother worked in the school cafeteria. After she was diagnosed with brain cancer, she begged the principal to give Lucky a janitorial position. The poor woman was desperate and dying. Lucky's father doesn't work – bad heart keeps him housebound. It's ironic really, Lucky's the breadwinner."

Althea shook her head and whispered, "Good Lord."

It was a frigid Friday night in mid-December when Althea heard a whining drone outside her house. After she loaded her few dishes in the dishwasher and headed upstairs, the whining, whirring sound was gone. She brushed her teeth and smoothed overnight moisturizer on her face. She settled in bed and opened Octavia Butler's *Fledgling*. She'd loved Octavia's time-traveling book, *Kindred*. The author's theme of surviving and thriving in adverse environments spoke to her. Octavia envisioned worlds where extraordinarily diverse people banded together to protect and sustain themselves. She wished Octavia were still alive. She would have liked to talk to her over a cup of tea.

Until the whining sound penetrated her consciousness, Althea was lost in the black vampire's journey to reclaim her place in her community. She rested the book face down, swung out of bed, and, shielded by the curtain, peeked outside. Between tree branches, the sky was black and cloudless, dimly lit by a waning crescent moon. Street lamps cast a yellowish glow.

Two sedans and a panel truck passed by. Althea saw nothing to concern her, and turned back to bed and book. But a few steps from the window, she stopped. A muffled whine grew louder. She tiptoed to the curtain and caught her breath.

A helmeted driver drove past on a Vespa scooter. With fascination and horror, Althea watched from the window as the rider disappeared and the whine subsided. And then, some moments later, a drone came from the far end of the road, growing louder, until the Vespa slowed in front of her house. Again and again, the scooter passed, slowed, passed from the other side. The knot in Althea's throat made it hard to swallow. Her heartbeat drummed in her ears. Hidden by the curtain, she stood transfixed for what seemed a long time until the drive-bys stopped. Her digital clock glowed green. 10:18.

In darkness, Althea descended the stairs. She shoved the kitchen table against the basement door. She checked and rechecked the locks. Then she found Henry's golf clubs and brought one upstairs. Neither

Octavia Butler nor *The Late Show with Stephen Colbert* kept Althea from fretting about the Vespa.

At four on Saturday morning, Althea gave up attempts at sleep. She took an extra long shower, dressed, went downstairs, and turned on every light. While she sipped coffee and flicked through her iPad, she told herself she was being ridiculous. But she couldn't let go of her sense of being stalked. She couldn't let go of her fear.

Something dropped on her head. As she skimmed fingers through her hair, she frowned. Not the time of year for insects. A bead of water splashed her iPad screen. Althea looked up. From a spreading stain on the ceiling overhead, another drop spattered her reading glasses. She grabbed her iPad and backed away. Water dripped in increasing frequency on the blue vinyl tablecloth. Althea's stomach lurched.

While she pulled the big stock pot from the cabinet and set it under the leak, her lower lip trembled, and tears welled in her eyes.

"For God's sake, stop!" She wasn't sure if she meant the leak or Lucky.

Her hands shook as she called Deondra and asked that Alonzo come over.

After Alonzo turned off the water and called a plumber, Althea packed some things and drove to Deondra's.

SHORTLY AFTER SHE ARRIVED, Deondra asked if she was up to babysitting. If she didn't mind, Deondra could use a few hours to go Christmas shopping without the kids.

Numb and exhausted, Althea rested her head on the sofa arm while the boys played *The Legend of Zelda* on their Nintendo. In response to her grandsons' attempts to gain her attention, she mumbled "Good job," or "That's great."

Alonzo's call had been bad news. "The plumber says your water pipes are corroded and the entire system has to be replaced. He says you really should update your sinks, toilets, and faucets, too. They're all more than thirty years old."

DEONDRA CALLED, "MOMS?"

Althea woke with a start. Her grandsons looked up from their Legos and smiled. The cable set-top box read 12:38 p.m. A pang of hunger clenched her stomach. She heard not only Deondra's voice, but Tamara's and Hettie's too. As her daughters filed into the rec room, Althea stood to face them.

"This is a surprise." Althea shook her head to clear it, still dazed and dull from her fitful sleep.

Hettie sat on the sofa with Althea. After Deondra told the boys to play in their rooms, she settled in a chair across from Tamara.

"Your house needs lots of work," Hettie said, light brown eyes filled with concern.

Deondra leaned forward. "After Daddy's funeral, Tamara said you needed time to work through your grief. She said we shouldn't hassle you about moving right away. When the time came, you'd make the right decision."

Althea tilted her head as she looked at Tamara, her baby, the quiet one. "You were right," she whispered.

Here, with her daughters around her, she felt safe. She let out a breath. The babies she and Henry cared for and protected grew to be fine, intelligent women who now wanted to care for and protect her. And Althea was ready to let them. The puckered dripping kitchen ceiling left a stain spreading through her brain.

"A home inspector should go over the house as soon as possible. That way, you'll know what needs to be repaired to make the house habitable. As long as you're facing major repairs, it makes sense to update the kitchen and bathrooms, and get the rooms painted. Alonzo says the roof and gutters should be replaced, and the furnace and water heater, too." Hettie hesitated. "Alonzo expects repairs and updating will run sixty-thousand dollars, maybe more."

"You can live here while the work's being done," Deondra said. "You can have the big bedroom at the end of the hall with its own bathroom. You don't have to worry about anything. Instead of going out to work, you can help us with the boys. They're thrilled to have you."

Althea sat back and wiped her eyes. She took slow breaths, aware of each inhalation and exhalation. Ever since Henry died, she'd felt off balance. She was so sad to lose Henry, and so tired of terrified sleepless nights. This wasn't the life she'd imagined. With their children grown and their pensions secure, she and Henry should have had time to reconnect, to rediscover the friendship and shared interests that brought them together a lifetime ago. But now that she finally got herself together, and had a good job where she was valued, their home, came down on her head. It betrayed her, like Henry did by dying. Deondra's words looped through her mind - 'You don't have to worry about anything.'

"I'll stay with you, Deondra," she whispered, barely able to speak the words.

"Moms?" Tamara asked, mouth tight. "Are you OK?"

Althea roused herself. "How much did Alonzo say the repairs will cost?"

"Sixty thousand or more. Homeowners insurance will cover the repairs, and Daddy's life insurance will cover the renovations," Hettie said. "Tomorrow I'll take you to the house to collect your things."

Althea nodded, then closed her eyes to speak to Henry. I tried to make it on my own, Henry, but I couldn't do it. I'm not the woman you married. I'm not the woman I thought I was. And now our house is in ruins. Did you know the house needed so much work?

Something inside broke. She needed a different path – the path of least resistance. She wanted to find the path of least resistance and follow it to the end of time.

ON MONDAY MORNING, while Deondra packed school lunches, the boys ate Lucky Charms with sliced bananas. Althea stared at the smiling leprechaun on the box. Lucky never smiled. She lingered over a second cup of coffee. What made her think she could handle a job and manage the house on her own? She felt like the Tin Man without a heart.

"Moms," Deondra said, "don't worry about your job. Just tell them you're sorry but you decided to spend more time with your family."

Althea had no memory of driving to McCleary Bunch Washington but once in the parking lot she found a spot near the back entrance. She grabbed the manila envelope holding her letter of resignation, and pulled her coat tight as she hurried through cold rain to the building.

A snowflake decal decorated the office door. When Althea entered, Sharon greeted her, "This is the first day I beat you in."

A red-nosed reindeer pulled a sleigh across Sharon's royal blue sweater. A sparkly white artificial Christmas tree took up one corner of the office, and a cheery blow-up snowman filled another. On Clayton's door, an evergreen wreath with a red bow emitted a clean piney smell.

"You've been busy," Althea said.

Her smile was sad as she realized how much she enjoyed working with Sharon, and how much she'd miss her after she quit. But Althea was done. She had nothing left to offer. She couldn't tell Sharon now, though. Maybe she wouldn't tell her at all. She'd leave that to the boss.

Clayton came out of his office. "Getting comfortable waltzing in at your leisure, I see," he said, eyebrows raised in a questioning look.

Althea glanced at the clock – 8:15. Her hours started at 8:30.

Clayton followed her gaze and smiled. "British humor."

AT THE END of the day, Althea drummed her fingers on her desk. She listened for Sharon's daily phone call to her sons to say she'd be home in twenty minutes. Finally, Sharon called, "See you tomorrow."

Althea rehearsed the words to tell Clayton she decided to resign. When she heard him take his coat off the hook, she hurried from her office.

"Do you have five minutes?" she asked.

Clayton's alarmed expression mirrored hers. "Tell me."

Althea cleared her throat, and cleared it again. Cold sweat beaded on her forehead. She ran the manila envelope through her fingers then handed it to him. Clayton's eyes bore into her soul.

"I decided to move in with my daughter and help with my

grandchildren." As soon as the words left her mouth, she wanted to take them back. She was so confused, so darned confused.

Clayton appeared more confused than Althea felt.

"No, not possible. You are not a nanny, you are a compliance coordinator." He handed back the envelope, and fixed his eyes on her. "What's really going on?"

Whatever response Althea anticipated, this was not one of them. She bit her lower lip. In a trembling voice, she answered, "Lucky drove his scooter past my house more than a dozen times Friday night. He frightens me. And my shower leaked through the ceiling into the kitchen and the house needs more than sixty thousand dollars of repairs, and I don't know what to do." She found herself sobbing for the first time since the funeral. "Henry wasn't supposed to die."

Clayton put his hands on her shoulders. "This time Lucky went too far. I'll talk to the principal about letting him go. But Althea, you're not the first person to face major home repairs. It's a royal pain, but you have to fix the house whether you quit your job or not. Won't you feel better with a paycheck coming in? Don't you think you're better off coming to work with people who admire you than spending your days washing grandchildren's laundry, and tripping over your daughter in her kitchen?"

Clayton's words made their way to her brain as if through a long tunnel.

Althea controlled her sobs and calmed herself.

"Don't let the principal to fire Lucky. Maybe you can talk to him. Tell him it's not mainstream to drive past people's houses at night."

"I can indeed," Clayton said. "Althea, don't decide today whether or not to keep the job. You need time to think things through. Don't make a rash decision." He gave her a conspiratorial look. "And please, don't mention any of this to Sharon."

Before she left the office, she got a text from Deondra – *can you buy berries, Cheerios, and milk on the way home?*

I see my future, Althea thought.

EVER SINCE HER October *Over hill* experience at Acme, Althea avoided shopping there. Now though, since it was most convenient, she steered her car into the lot. After she parked, she locked the car and scanned the lot, feeling paranoid. No Vespa.

"Hey, Mrs. Taylor," a booming voice called from outside Coffee Town, the new coffee shop on the adjoining strip.

Althea recognized the boy and his friends from the high school. She smiled and waved. The boys waved back, even as they hooted and shoved each other in fun. She'd miss this, being recognized and recognizing the kids. As she crossed the automatic door into the grocery store, she felt better than she had over the weekend. Her talk with Clayton helped a little.

In the produce section, the berries looked nasty so she selected six green bananas. She chose the big box of Cheerios – Lord knows those children will finish a box in two days. As she heaved a gallon of milk into her cart, *Over hill, over dale, as we hit the dusty trail . . .* drifted from the snacks aisle. She steered the cart toward the safety of the checkout lanes. But before she reached the end of the aisle, Lucky rounded the corner and stopped.

Over hill, over dale, as we hit the dusty trail . . . After a pause, he said, "It's your turn."

Althea fought back her anxiety. She took a deep breath and in a soft voice sang, *And the caissons, go rolling, along.*

"There." Lucky pushed past, marching behind his cart singing random lyrics.

Althea decided to wait to get in line until after Lucky checked out. She studied the magazine rack while listening for his song. When she realized a stock clerk was watching, she tossed an *Oprah* in her cart. Finally, she decided it was safe – no sight or sound of Lucky. After she swiped her credit card, she pushed her cart to the store entrance.

Through the plate glass window, Althea saw Lucky pressed against her car, surrounded by the boys she waved to on her way in. She inched back into the store and watched.

The blond kid straddled Lucky's Vespa. Another boy wore Lucky's helmet. Lucky leaned against her car with hunched shoulders and fists clenched around two grocery bags.

No, no, no, it's not your battle, Althea told herself. Those are kids from school. They won't hurt him. I don't need to get involved. But even as those thoughts went through her mind, her feet carried her out the door and through the parking to her car.

"Hey, Mrs. Taylor," the blond boy said, voice cheery. "Lucky promised to let us ride his scooter, but now he won't give us the key." He turned to Lucky. "Come on, Lucky, I won't hurt your scooter. It would be mainstream to let me take a ride."

"No one can ride but me," Lucky said. His face had the same blank expression as always, but Althea felt his fear.

"Look, here's my license." The boy pulled out his wallet and showed it to Lucky. "Mrs. Taylor wants a ride, too."

Lucky took his eyes off the Vespa and glanced at Althea.

"Now boys, give Lucky his helmet and get off his bike. I'll see you tomorrow." She trembled, but wasn't afraid.

"You spoil all the fun," the blond kid said in a friendly tone. "See you tomorrow."

As the boys walked away, one called, "We'll take that ride another time, Lucky."

Althea faced Lucky. "After I put my groceries in the trunk, I'm going to Coffee Town. Would you like to come?"

"My mother says coffee's bad for me," he said in his toneless way.

"Come along. I'll get you a hot chocolate. Do you think that would be okay with your mother?"

"My mother's dead," Lucky said.

"Well then she probably won't mind."

With eyes cast down, Lucky tucked his groceries in the Vespa's saddlebags then shuffled behind Althea to Coffee Town. He stood too close while she ordered, his eyes fixed on the cash register.

"A small coffee with steamed milk, and a large hot chocolate. And please drop a few ice cubes in the hot chocolate." She pulled a five from her wallet.

"I have money," Lucky said.

"Since I invited you, I'll pay. Will you find us a table?"

After she set down the drinks, Lucky licked his lips and pried off the hot chocolate top. Before he took a sip, he stirred until the ice cubes melted. Althea held her cup with both hands and inhaled the milky smell. When she noticed Lucky imitating her, she smiled.

His eyes were on the table when he said, "Why do they say this is Coffee Town? It isn't a town, it's a store."

"It's a name that's easy for people to remember," Althea said.

"Lucky's a name that's easy for people to remember. But I'm not a leprechaun and Lucky's not my real name. My real name is Liam."

"Then I'll call you Liam," Althea said, surprised at his words.

"When Santa rings his bell, my mother said I should drop a quarter in his pot. A quarter is the same as two dimes and a nickel. One time I put in three dimes, that's thirty cents," Liam said. "Thirty cents is more than a quarter." After each sip, he stirred his cup.

"That's very generous. I'm sure your mother's happy when you give Santa money."

"My mother's dead," Liam said.

"My mother's dead, too." Althea checked her watch and pushed back her chair. "I have to be going, Liam. My family's waiting. Are you safe to drive home?"

"I got my helmet." He didn't look up.

Althea loved Deondra and Alonzo. She loved her grandsons. But she wouldn't last a whole month living with them, let alone forever.

The house where she and Henry raised their family needed extensive work, inside and out, and the contractor estimated repairs would take four months, maybe five. The timing was actually good, Hettie told her. It would be ready by late spring, the best time to put a house on the market.

Althea had come to accept that the only sensible decision was to sell the house. It was too big for one person, and the thought of mowing the lawn, shoveling snow, cleaning the gutters, and being responsible for everything that could go wrong made her dizzy.

WITHOUT TELLING THE GIRLS, Althea spent two afternoons studying listings for apartments and another two afternoons checking out the best prospects.

Only after Althea put down a deposit on a lovely two bedroom apartment with a den and a patio, did she announce she would soon have a new address. It was close enough to walk to McCleary Bunch Washington High School, and just a short drive to Deondra's. Move-in was the first Saturday in January.

THE DAY BEFORE WINTER BREAK, Althea brought in two home-baked sweet potato pies. As soon as she entered the office, Sharon called, "Merry Christmas. Ho, ho, ho." The red Santa hat perched on Sharon's head matched the Santa hat on her sweatshirt.

"Merry Christmas." Althea gave Sharon a pie.

After she hung her coat, she gave Clayton the other pie, and a card in which she'd tucked her resignation letter with a red slash through it and *NOT* written in black magic marker.

"So it will be a Merry Christmas," Clayton whispered. "You made the right decision. Sharon and I would be lost without you."

He followed her to the reception area and stood beside her at the coffee pot. Althea looked for her cup, but it was gone.

"Did you see my cup?" Althea asked as she bit into a tree-shaped cookie covered with green sprinkles.

"Maybe you left it on your desk," Sharon said, her voice a model of innocence.

Althea moved to her office and stopped short. A large cup from Coffee Town sat in the middle of her blotter.

"Where did this come from?"

"Your secret admirer," Clayton said.

Sharon held her hands out palms up.

From the hall, barely louder than *Holly Jolly Christmas* coming from Sharon's CD player, Althea heard, *Over hill, over dale, as we hit the dusty trail . . .*

A pasty face pressed against the office door window. Before it disappeared, Althea raised the Coffee Town cup in salute.

～

THE HALLS WERE empty when Althea locked the office at 4 o'clock. Kids, staff, Clayton, Sharon, everyone had rushed out to begin winter break. When she left the building, the sky was growing dark on this shortest day of the year.

As she crossed the parking lot, Liam waited by his scooter. No one else was around. She felt the familiar lurch in her stomach and drumming of her heart. Her impulse was to hurry to her car before he noticed, but she stopped, caught her breath, and walked across the asphalt toward him.

"Merry Christmas, Liam, and Happy New Year," she said. "Thank you for the coffee."

"We come back January 4th. No school for two weeks then right back to work on January 4th," he said, eyes fixed on the scooter seat.

"Yes," Althea said. "See you then." She started for her car, then stopped and sang, *Over hill, over dale, we will hit the dusty trail . . .*

Liam's eyes met hers as he sang, *And the caissons go rolling along.*

6

THE DECLINE AND FALL

Gloria Larsen opened her watery eyes to sunshine streaming through curtains. In the middle of her living room, she lay on the hospital bed the doctor insisted she buy after that silly fainting spell at church.

Tried to put me in a nursing home. Not me, no sir. I have my own home right here. She kicked off the tangled blanket and rested her arm under her head. Her wrist felt like a twig. Before she got up, Gloria took a moment to plan her day. Now, what day was it?

The Ryan family, Marty, Cynthia, and the boys, stopped by with chicken soup, peach pie, and vanilla ice cream on Sunday. Gloria finished the soup and pie yesterday - Monday. So, today was Tuesday, Senior Suppers day.

Yesterday, Janice, the Senior Suppers lady, called to say Sam couldn't deliver anymore. That was disappointing. Sam was great for bringing in the mail. Gloria hoped the new Senior Suppers driver would be as courteous and efficient.

She grabbed the bedrail and rolled to her stomach, anticipating the jolt of knee and hip pain when her feet hit the floor. What no one tells you about getting old is that everything hurts. Well, she made it eighty-eight years, she guessed she could make it another day. As she steadied herself, her hand brushed the wet sheet but she ignored it as well as the damp gown flapping around her legs. She reached for her walker, and clumped to the kitchen. A cup of tea to start the day.

HELEN WITT PUSHED THE GLOVES, umbrella, and overdue library books off the passenger seat of her red Ford Escort.

At forty-two, Helen had experienced her share of bad luck. Two years ago, she was hanging a Halloween wreath in the reception area at work, and fell off the step ladder. She filed for workers compensation without success. Finally, her mother hired an attorney who got her a structured settlement with small monthly payments. The money wasn't enough to live on but she never had to work again, or listen to her mother bitch if she asked to borrow a few bucks.

Just last week, Helen was watching Dr. Phil when her mother, a heavy-set woman of sixty-five, marched in, ripped the remote out of her fist, and turned off the TV. It was unexpected and frightening.

For no good reason, her mother berated her.

"Get off your duff and do something with your life. I won't have you sprawling on my sofa all day."

"It's not like I have to work," Helen answered, flailing for the remote. "What do you expect me to do?"

Mother kept the remote behind her back. "Volunteer, deliver Senior Suppers, do something. You're forty-two-years-old, Helen. Grow up, and get yourself together. I'm not going to be around forever."

Cancer, brain tumor, heart failure . . . Helen's mood brightened. The house would be hers.

"Are you saying you're ill?"

"I'm saying I handed in my retirement papers and as soon as I sell this house, I'm moving to an active adult community in Florida. The minimum age is fifty-five."

"You can't sell the house. Where will I go?" Helen wailed.

"That's your problem. You're an adult."

Mother walked away with the remote, and Helen didn't find it for two days.

The next day, Mother drove her to the Senior Suppers Office and handed her a pen. Helen dutifully filled out the volunteer application. What else could she do?

When Helen received an email to appear for Senior Suppers orientation, Mother bought her a gorgeous purple track suit from Walmart, and paid for a full tank of gas. Helen supposed her mother put her on the county list for subsidized housing, too.

Now, she turned the key and her aging Escort's engine sputtered to life. Her heart drummed with excitement. Today was the first day of her life as a Senior Suppers volunteer. Just yesterday, she read on Facebook: *Only a life lived for others is a life worthwhile.* Helen thought Ben Stein said that.

AFTER A CUP OF TEA, Gloria clumped to the bathroom. The toilet was the best place to put on her therapeutic shoes. Her left hand gripped the safety bar while she reached with her right to squeeze her feet in the shoes. Toes were the tough part. Big toes angled into second toes and bunions jutted at the joint. But once she wiggled in the ball of her foot, it was easy to jam in her heel and close the Velcro straps.

While Gloria brushed her teeth, she studied herself in the mirror. She'd always been a beauty, with fair skin, blue eyes that inspired young men to poetry, and wavy blonde hair. All four years of high school she was elected prom queen, and at the University of Kansas where she studied home economics, she was crowned Miss Hay Capitol. Gloria sighed. When Navy Lieutenant Gunnar Larsen came home after World War II, she was smitten. That night at the drive-in, she supposed she let things go too far, but she'd been filled with patriotic spirit.

They moved to Philadelphia and lived together well enough for forty-five years, even though the pregnancy that led to their hurried marriage ended in miscarriage. They were never blessed with children. Gunnar's job with Burroughs Corporation took him all over the world. Gloria filled those solitary days nurturing flowers, ornamentals, vegetables, and herbs on the grounds of the house they bought in 1957.

When Gunnar died twenty years ago, he left her alone but well provided for. She rarely thought about him anymore.

Gloria fumbled with the belt to her flannel robe and eventually got it knotted. She must do a load of wash today, and tend the garden.

HANDS ON HIPS, Helen watched Janice, the Senior Suppers manager, load meals in the back of the Escort.

After Janice shut the hatchback, she turned to Helen. "Your senior, Mrs. Larsen, Gloria, lives alone. She's quite a talker."

"No problemo," Helen said.

Blonde, bubbly Janice smiled at Helen. "You can make a difference in this person's life."

That's all Helen ever wanted — to make a difference, to be loved, *to dream the impossible dream, to fight the unbeatable foe, to bear with unbearable sorrow, to run where the brave dare not go.*

As she pulled out of the parking lot and thumped onto the road, she sang with the radio, *All you need is love.* Maybe Mother was right. It felt good to be out and about, doing meaningful work.

With one eye on the road and one eye on the directions, Helen almost missed Rose Lane. When she pulled the steering wheel hard right, she scraped the curb. A woman on the sidewalk with two fox-faced dogs jumped back and gave Helen an angry glare, but really, it wasn't on purpose. My bad, she mouthed to the woman, tapping her middle finger on the window.

After she found the address and parked in the driveway, Helen thought she'd entered an arboretum. The front yard was lush, overgrown really, with thorny roses and other colorful plants. The house was robin's egg blue, and surrounded by shrubs.

She hopped out, straightened her top - she wanted to make a good impression - and piled the meals in what Mother called a lazy man's load. While she waited at the front door, her foot tapped to her favorite song - *If you liked it then you should have put a ring on it.*

A bent woman opened the door a crack. Her stunning blue eyes sparkled from a pale wrinkled face, framed by wispy white hair.

"Senior Suppers," Helen sang in a happy voice.

"Come in."

The old lady's voice quivered with palsy. Her words came out creaky, forced to the surface with pain, like a baby's first tooth.

Helen pushed the door with her rump and swung inside, balancing the boxes like the leaning Tower of Pizza.

"You almost knocked me over," the old lady said.

The house smelled stagnant and pissy, the furniture needed dusting, and it was too dark for Helen. She must open the windows, and let the sun shine in. On a faded Oriental rug in the middle of the living room, a hospital bed stood in disarray.

"Where shall I put your meals?" Helen sang.

The woman motioned to the right. The kitchen was orderly though not what Helen would call clean.

"Would you like a cup of tea?" the old lady asked.

"That would be lovely," Helen said. "Are you ready for today's meal? I'll put the others in the fridge."

Helen looked for something to wipe the table. Since the dishrag on the faucet was stiff and cruddy, she brushed off crumbs with her sleeve before she placed the Styrofoam container with tomato soup, crackers, ketchup-covered meatloaf, and mashed potatoes on the table.

The old woman's hands trembled when she handed Helen the cup of tea, and Helen feared she'd get splashed. But after she accepted the cup and saucer, the woman, Mrs. Larsen, moved around the table and successfully dropped in her chair. She pried open the Styrofoam lid and licked her lips.

"This is fine, dear. Sam was never one to set my plate." Soup spilled off the spoon before she got it in her mouth, but she seemed not to notice. She glanced at Helen and said, "Don't let me keep you."

"You have a nice house, Mrs. Larsen."

"Call me Gloria."

"I'm Helen. Gloria, do you live alone?"

"For the past twenty years, since Gunnar died."

Helen furrowed her brow to look sympathetic.

"How do you manage? Groceries, doctor appointments, and such."

Gloria sipped soup from the container. "People on this street watch out for each other. A young family, the Ryans, used to live next door. They moved away but still drop by every week. Todd, the oldest boy, he's something else. When he was little, he loved to sit in my car and pretend to drive. We bought the Cadillac new in 1986. Ocean Blue. Gunnar said the color matched my eyes."

"Like your house."

Gloria chopped the meatloaf with the plastic fork. A glob of mashed potato spattered on the floor.

"I promised Todd the car when he turned sixteen. Now he's sixteen but his father says there's too much paperwork, and I should keep it. Keep it? I haven't driven for years."

"Of course not, it's too dangerous. People drive like lunatics, and they're so rude. Where do you keep your car?"

"In the garage. Goodness, it doesn't have but 23,000 miles on it. Do you want to see it?"

When Gloria smiled, her pink nose and tiny teeth reminded Helen of Fluffy, the little kitten she had as a child until she dropped him in the toilet to teach him to swim, and he drowned.

She followed Gloria through the laundry room into the garage. The car was covered in dust thick enough to write your name and surrounded by a big mess of newspapers, paint cans, and rusted tools. Still, Helen recognized quality when she saw it.

"It's dreamy. Such a beautiful car with no one to drive it."

Gloria nodded, from satisfaction or palsy, Helen couldn't tell. But she could tell that Gloria was feeble, barely able to fend for herself, all alone in this lovely old house with that lovely old car. All the house, the car, and Gloria needed was a little cleaning up.

When Helen followed Gloria back into the house, she noticed the wet stain on the hospital bed.

"Why don't I change those sheets and start a load of wash before I go?" Helen said.

"That would be nice, Dear," Gloria answered in her quivery voice.

After Helen removed the pissy sheets, she pushed the bed into sunlight to dry out the mattress. Before she started a load of wash, she had to dig out a bunch of towels stuck like cement to the washer tub. She added vinegar to the detergent to clear the mildew smell.

As she scanned the first floor rooms, Helen knew her work was cut out for her. She turned to Gloria with her most sincere smile.

"You're too pretty for that old robe," Helen said. "Let's get you into something fresh."

"I need help with the stairs. Would it be too much to ask you to stay while I have a bath?" Gloria asked.

An hour later, Helen, face flushed with satisfaction, backed out of Gloria's driveway. Such a gorgeous house and much too big for that poor old thing, living all alone. She needs someone to take care of her. Why shouldn't it be me?

ON A BRIGHT SEPTEMBER MORNING, Gloria worked in the back yard, wearing garden gloves and the floppy hat Gunnar bought in Guadalajara. She tapped her housecoat pocket to feel for her comfort-coated floral scissors.

Helen insisted she should pay a boy to prune but Gloria enjoyed tending to her plants, and she didn't want a child near her belladonna shrub. She had nurtured the belladonna - *pretty lady* - for sixty years, since Gunnar planted it. Of course, the leaves and fruit were poisonous, but the plant was lovely, with shiny black berries nestled in green starfish-shaped calyxes. Bell-shaped purple flowers sprang from the stalks.

Gloria took care not to touch the belladonna barehanded. She clipped the closest branch, then the next, and the next until her fingers grew stiff. The sun glowed pink in the cloudless sky. A bee buzzed so near she felt the caress of its wings. When a breeze made her shiver, she turned to go inside. Helen would arrive soon.

Each day Helen came, Gloria liked to get something accomplished. Today, she planned to ask Helen to help look through her jewelry boxes. She hadn't held the necklaces, bracelets, brooches, and rings in years - baubles Gunnar brought her each time he returned from a trip.

MONDAYS, Tuesdays, and Thursdays, Helen delivered Senior Suppers to Gloria. Mother stopped nagging, thank God. She put the house on the market but Helen wasn't concerned. She felt confident she'd soon have a much nicer place to live than her mother's shabby rambler.

On the drive to Gloria's, the Escort's engine light flicked on. Helen smelled something burning but put the bad thought out of her mind. Instead, she imagined Gloria's smile when she pulled out two packs of chocolate mini-donuts that found their way into her purse when the clerk looked the other way. Gloria's groceries jostled on the passenger side floor - milk, eggs, balsamic vinaigrette salad dressing, Barry's Dublin tea, and strawberry yogurt. Gloria gave her more than enough money, so Helen added paper towels, laundry detergent, Pepsi, and Cinnamon Toast Crunch, certain Gloria would be appreciative. As she pulled in the driveway, her heart gave a happy flutter.

She rang the doorbell and called, "Gloria!"

Arms loaded, Helen waited on the porch for the scrunch-clump of Gloria's walker. She tapped her foot. When she told Gloria she should have her own key, Gloria said in her quivery voice, I'm not ready to do that. What, did Gloria think she'd break in and rob her?

Helen hummed *See you in September.* Come on, come on, she willed until Gloria cracked open the door. She squeezed past the old lady and put the groceries on the kitchen table.

"We needed detergent and paper towels, so I bought them. I love Pepsi, don't you?"

She put most of the change from Gloria's fifty-dollar bill on the table. When Gloria slid into her chair, Helen curtsied and with flourish, pulled the packages of chocolate mini-donuts from her purse.

"For our tea, Madame."

The kitchen was spotless. When she opened the refrigerator, neatly stacked plastic containers filled the middle shelf. A quart of orange juice stood in the door rack next to a jar of olives. A baggie with celery and carrots sat on the bottom shelf.

"What's this?" Helen asked, with accusation.

"The Ryans stopped by yesterday with some home-cooked meals." Gloria's voice sounded like a creaky chair. "We had such a nice day. Todd raked the yard and washed my windows. Cynthia and Marty took me for a drive - it was wonderful." Her blue eyes gleamed above her sunken cheeks. "Todd drove the Cadillac around the block a few times. Marty says it's in good shape, considering."

Gloria bit into a donut and glanced at Helen. "These are delicious."

Helen jammed her last donut into her mouth. It tasted like chocolate flavored sawdust. "I don't know why you need Senior Suppers with all this food. Why don't you get a home health aide?"

"Because I have you, dear," Gloria said.

For the interminable trip to the second floor, Helen held her hand against the small of Gloria's back. In the dingy bedroom, Gloria dropped into the straight-backed chair by the vanity. Helen wrinkled her nose, trying to identify the smell – like dog dirt on an old shoe.

"Will you bring me my jewelry boxes?" Gloria pointed to her bureau where necklaces hung from hooks in a large cherry box. A small tarnished silver box shaped like a coffin sat next to it.

Helen brought over the large jewelry box, but couldn't take her eyes off the little silver one. She cradled it reverently, as if in adoration. A bird and butterfly glided through flowers etched across its domed top. When Gloria held out her hands for it, Helen set it on the vanity out of Gloria's reach.

"That little box was my wedding gift from Gunnar. A place for your rings, he said. But I think of it as the casket for the child we lost."

"I think it's exquisite. If it makes you sad, why do you keep it?"

"For sentimental reasons, I suppose."

Helen opened windows, and coughed when dust broke loose from yellowed lace curtains. When she circled back, she moved the silver casket to Gloria's reaching hands, then sat on the bed. It was surprisingly comfortable. After she washed the sheets and freshened the comforter, why, the bed would suit her fine.

Gloria glanced over and sneezed.

"Do you have family, Gloria?"

"None living."

"What will you do with your things?"

"You mean when I die? The house goes to Cynthia and Marty. With three boys, they'll get great use from it. And the children's education will be covered by my savings."

Helen's heart dropped. Didn't the Ryan family have their own home? Still, Gloria seemed in good health. No reason to worry. There was plenty of time.

THE THING about these Senior Suppers people, Gloria thought, is they wear on a person.

The November sun shone as bright and warm as summer. In the backyard, Gloria clipped oval leaves and shiny black berries from her belladonna plant and dropped them in the pocket of the blue-checked housecoat Helen picked up at Walmart.

Each time Helen ran errands, she bought more things than Gloria put on the list. As if I'd ever display plastic flowers in my house! And those coffee mugs marked *Friends 4 Ever* - what was Helen thinking? The mug was too heavy, and she did not like the taste of tea in it. Last visit, Helen asked if they should get a natural or artificial tree, and what did Gloria want for Christmas?

What Gloria wanted was a new Senior Suppers driver, thank you very much. Yet, Helen was so willing. They made progress organizing Gloria's things - jewelry, fine china, the wall-to-wall books in the library, and Gunnar's collection of recordings going back to 1930. What a time to be alive!

Gloria plucked the last shiny black berry from the branch. She must put them away before Helen arrived. She hoped Helen wouldn't pester her about the car again.

HELEN'S CAR sputtered into the driveway. Joe, her mother's mechanic, said the Escort was dying, with oil in the radiator and radiator fluid in the engine. Car's not worth the cost of repair. Not with a cracked block.

Cracked block! Joe's block is cracked is what Helen thought. She stomped to Gloria's door.

"I'm here," she trilled and put on her happy face.

No need to spread gloom, her mother always said. Yet, how could Helen keep up her visits without a car? Meeting Gloria had been great. Helen was making a difference, helping an old lady, and, truth be told, had accumulated a nice little pile of gifts - a necklace, a shawl, *Pickwick Papers* by Dickens in good condition considering its copyright was 1842. She felt certain she could sell it on eBay. Helen felt certain the silver jewelry box would be hers, too.

Her mother had a contract on the house. In January, she'd move away and abandon her, with no concern for what Helen would do then. In Helen's dream of dreams, she would move in with Gloria. Then she'd tell her mother, *Good riddance to bad rubbish.* But first, I need Gloria's Cadillac, and then, I need Gloria's house.

When Gloria opened the door, Helen lit up her face and sang, "You look beautiful! The housecoat brings out the blue in your eyes! I brought an emery board and peach nail polish. I'm going to give you a manicure!"

When she entered, Helen nodded in satisfaction. Only a slight smell of urine remained. While Gloria clopped to the kitchen and turned on the burner for tea, Helen pulled the wet sheets off the hospital bed, dropped them in the washer, and took clean ones from the dryer.

"Did you bring those little chocolate donuts for tea?" Gloria called.

"Not today. I've had such a bad day."

While she made up the hospital bed, Helen glanced into the kitchen. Gloria stood by the window, as translucent as a ghost. When she turned, a sunbeam glinted off her eyes. After Helen fluffed the pillows, she headed to the kitchen and collapsed in a chair. With head in hands, she sobbed.

"Joe says my car's dying and it's not worth fixing. The block is cracked. I don't even know what that means."

"Oh my," Gloria said, delicately sipping tea.

"Please let me borrow your car while I figure out what to do."

"I'm sorry, Helen, I promised the car to Todd."

Helen's plump face was wet and blotchy. "I just need to borrow it for a week. I'll get Joe to inspect it and make sure it's safe for Todd. I know. Let's take it out for a ride, see how it drives. We can go wherever you want, and stop for ice cream on the way home."

"Getting the car in tip-top shape is a good idea," Gloria said, "and so is ice cream." She licked her lips.

Helen followed Gloria into the garage - another room to clean. Gloria flipped a switch, and the garage door creaked open, barely high enough for the Cadillac to pass under.

When Helen put the key in the starter, the engine groaned to life. She jockeyed the gearshift into Drive and they lurched down the driveway. The brakes were powerful and sticky and the steering wheel had so much play Helen felt like she was driving an electric bumper car at the carnival. As they bumped into the street, Helen turned the radio dial. Thumping bass notes pounded hard rap music - *Give me two-pair, I need two-pair, Big Boy . . .*

"Gunnar and I prefer classical music," Gloria said.

Helen pressed buttons until she found her favorite easy listening station. She sang along - *I hope you still feel small when you stand beside the ocean. Whenever one door closes, I hope one more opens . . .*

"Well, that's a pretty tune," Gloria said.

Gloria smelled much better these days - her clothes of lavender detergent, her hair of fruity shampoo. But in the close quarters of the car, Helen smelled decay, like sodden leaves in the woods after a storm.

In the passenger seat, Gloria sat wide-eyed and smiling, and Helen felt it was only a matter of time until she worked her way into Gloria's heart . . . and home.

GLORIA FELT it was only a matter of time until she worked Helen out of her life. Oh, the girl served a purpose. The house was clean and tidy, Gloria got regular baths, and she had to admit, Helen did a decent manicure. She listened for the Cadillac to pull into the driveway, just as she'd listened for Gunnar all those years.

Evenings, they took long walks. After dinner, they listened to Caruso sing *Pagliacci* on 78 rpms and took turns reading from *The Decline and Fall of the Roman Empire*. She remembered it well. *In the*

second century of the Christian era, the Empire of Rome comprehended the
fairest part of the earth, and the most civilized portion of mankind.

Now that the Cadillac was in good running condition and the
licensing up-to-date, Gloria hoped Janice would find someone halfway
intelligent to deliver her Senior Suppers.

The girl is insipid, Gloria thought, painfully insipid. And Helen
stole from her - money, baubles, knick-knacks, and costume jewelry -
but Gloria pretended not to notice. Better to let Helen dig her own
grave.

With her left hand squeezed into one of the yellow rubber gloves
Helen bought at Walmart, Gloria took a plastic salad bowl from the
kitchen cabinet. The refrigerator door took three yanks to open. Gloria
leaned over her walker to reach the bag of chopped spinach Helen
bought the other day. I love spinach, Helen had said. Today she would
make Helen a nice spinach salad, how lovely.

With her gloved hand, Gloria pulled a dish from behind the toaster,
where she'd put aside the berries and leaves from the belladonna
plant.

She chopped the leaves, brushed the pieces into the salad bowl,
added spinach, and fluffed the greens with a fork. She dropped the
shiny black berries on top. They would be sweet and lend a touch of
color. I always like a taste of fruit with my salad, she would say, I
thought you might, too.

Today is the day Gloria would give Helen everything she ever
dreamed of - the car, the house, government bonds, and the casket-
shaped jewelry box she so often admired. It hurt to laugh.

Where is that salad dressing? Gloria jerked her walker to the
refrigerator. When she yanked the door open, the small of her back
sent alarming pain radiating down her right buttocks and through her
thigh, to burn in the recesses of her withered calf. She slipped to her
knees, slumped over the walker frame.

WHEN HELEN, singing *Good Morning Sunshine*, entered the kitchen
through the garage, Gloria raised her head.

"Oh my," Helen said. "Dear God."

Eyes wide, Gloria gazed at her with ghostly skin and desperation. The old woman's arms hung on the walker as she slumped on her knees in a spreading pool of urine. Helen rushed to her, flung aside the walker, and grasped Gloria in a hug. She dragged Gloria to the living room with super-human strength. With a one-two-three, she hoisted Gloria up on her hospital bed.

"I'm ok," Gloria whispered, so low Helen could barely hear.

"I'm calling 9-1-1," Helen sang. She turned her head to smile. Gloria was a goner.

"No, no," Gloria said, "No ambulance. I'm not leaving my house. My sciatica flared up, that's all. Lord knows, you don't live eighty-eight years without some discomfort."

A vein pulsed blue across Gloria's forehead and her gnarled hands clenched in fists.

"Let me get you out of those wet clothes. After I clean up the mess, we'll see how you feel."

Not yet, Helen thought, don't die yet. I haven't had enough time to make you change your will. I do so much for you. I'm the one who helps you. I'm the one you need.

"I'll be fine. I just need a minute," Gloria said, voice quivery.

Helen pinched herself. This was better than she planned, more than she prayed for. God is good. Helen was a month away from losing her home, and today, Gloria desperately needed her. She mopped the floor, put Gloria's wet clothes in the washer, and cleaned the old lady with a warm cloth.

After Gloria turned on her side and shimmied to the floor, Helen dressed her in a fresh housecoat, and helped her totter to the kitchen.

Helen would promise to care for Gloria, and move in so Gloria could stay in her home. In return, all she wanted was a place to live, a car to drive, a little spending money, and gold jewelry was always nice. Of course, she would say, you must take care of Todd and his brothers. I feel the same way.

THE STABBING PAIN took away Gloria's breath, yet it was a godsend - the perfect opportunity to tell Helen how much she depended on her, needed her, thought of her as the daughter she never had. She leaned on Helen to drag her feet to the kitchen.

"I'll brew us some tea," Gloria said. "I made you a beautiful salad for lunch."

"You're so good to me. Are you sure you're okay? Do you need your meds?" Helen asked.

"No, I'm okay. But I'd like you to run upstairs and bring down the small jewelry box. Then we'll have lunch."

It took every ounce of strength for Gloria to lift Helen's salad and carry it to the table. With tiny beads of sweat forming on her upper lip, Gloria backed into her chair, exhausted. She listened to Helen rummaging around upstairs. The girl never missed an opportunity to go through Gloria's things. Footsteps pounded down the steps.

"Your little jewelry box," Helen sang and placed it in front of Gloria.

"I want you to have it. You've been a great help, and this is dear to me, as you are," Gloria said, pushing it towards Helen.

Helen trembled. Her hooded eyes glistened and her pouty lips were pink and puckered. Gloria thought of Sheba, the golden retriever she had for twelve years, shaking with delight at the prospect of a bone. She would throw Helen a bone, why not?

"I've decided to change my will. After I die, I want you to have the house and car. Gunnar was very wise with money. Between social security and the return on our investments, I've lived very well over the years, and I expect you will too. Of course, I have commitments to the Ryan boys. I intend to give Todd money to buy a new car and leave money for all three boys to go to college."

HELEN COULD NOT BELIEVE her ears. Her dream came true. All she ever wanted was to help people, to make a difference, to live a good life in a nice house. Across the table, Gloria's hands shook so much she couldn't bring her teacup to her lips.

"Thank you," Helen said. "I'll take care of you. We'll go for long rides on nice days, and we'll buy a big TV to watch movies when it rains."

It will be so easy to take away Gloria's pain after she changes the will, Helen thought. A slip, a fall, a pillow pressed gently on her face. *No autopsy, she wouldn't want that. I'm her only survivor. Yes, she would like her ashes strewn over her garden.* Helen smiled and reached for the salad.

"You're such a beautiful person," Helen said.

GLORIA WISHED Helen could help her up. The pain in her hip was excruciating. But after Helen finished the belladonna berry salad, she staggered from the table and collapsed on the floor, blocking the front door. Before the convulsions became so unpleasant, the putrid smell was unexpected, Helen sang to herself in a slurred voice — *Let the sun shine, let the sun shine in.* Let the sun shine in, indeed.

There lay Helen, sprawled across the threshold, her essence spreading through the house, leaving its impression on Gloria's things.

Gloria pulled herself up and clumped to the chair by the telephone. She sat for a moment to catch her breath and plan the rest of her day. First, call 9-1-1 and get that thing removed. Then, call Janice and ask her to assign another driver.

Gloria sighed and wished Helen brought those little chocolate donuts today.

"THE DECLINE AND FALL" was runner-up in the *Saturday Evening Post* 2013 Great American Fiction Contest, published by *Saturday Evening Post* at saturdayeveningpost.com, December 17, 2012.

7

WITHERED HOPE

I f you ever drove those back roads in Jersey through the Pine Barrens, you know what I'm talking about. God almighty, they wind and curve, and it's dark as hell when the sun goes down. That's how it was last night. No moon, heavy clouds, black except for the dull beam from my headlights. Swampy smell to the air. Scrub trees and brush all along the narrow road. Mosquitoes too.

A big-ass deer jumped out of nowhere, hit the front of my car, and crashed into the windshield. I slammed the brakes, and my head hit the steering wheel. It's a wonder I wasn't killed. I want to tell you, I was shaking. Damn thing flew into the scrub, but left my windshield covered in black blood, and my front end smashed like I hit a Mack truck. I drove that Olds for thirty years, got about 8 miles to the gallon. Now, it's totaled for sure.

I managed to steer the car onto grass, so at least I wasn't a target for other cars. Like I said, my hands were shaking, my head hurt, and my heart beat like the bass drum my son played in marching band.

I'd been out deep-sea fishing off Longport with Bill Bianchi, my boss at the transit agency. I've fixed SEPTA bus motors since I finished high school. We got sunburned as hell, drank a case of Bud, and caught three bass and five blue fish. Not bad. I hope Bill enjoys his half of the catch because mine is stewing in the Oldsmobile trunk.

So anyway, I'm shook up, right? It's so dark I can't see a thing outside, and I'm smelling gasoline, dead deer, and that rotten egg smell you get near the seashore. I'm sitting there trying to get my bearings, you know what I mean, and something drips from my forehead, down my cheek, all the way to the side of my mouth. I tasted thick salty blood, mine or the deer's, I didn't know.

My head knocked the steering wheel crooked. Old cars don't have airbags, you know. I jammed my shoulder against the door to open it, and stepped into fog thick as soup. Right away, I puked up sour beer and potato chips. Let me tell you, I don't recommend it.

It must have been after nine. It was that clammy cool it gets at night. Thanks to my pukefest, I wasn't drunk anymore, but I was messed up. So I'm looking around, wondering what to do. The car is wrecked, a front tire is blown, and I don't see lights, houses, signs, nothing. I patted my pockets, but couldn't find my cell phone. Then, I heard rustling from where the deer landed, and went over to check it out. The deer was on its side, kicking, then stopped. If you didn't know better, you'd think it was human. I felt sorry for it, even though it wrecked my car. No one should die scared and helpless in a heap along the road.

I'm standing there thinking about the deer when two red lights like Christmas tree bulbs float towards me from the pines. Talk about your heart in your throat! I thought it was the freaking Jersey devil! I about ripped the door off the Olds, jumped in, shut the door, and closed my eyes. I'm not ashamed to say I made the sign of the cross. That must have worked because when I looked, the red eyes were gone. I remembered it was Halloween and wondered if someone was playing a trick one me. But no one was around.

After a while I got out of the car. The fog was like being inside a a cloud. I was shivering, gulping air, and ready to cry. Right, grown men don't cry, like I don't know that. You weren't there. Anyway, I'm leaning against the car and praying my ass off when hazy yellow headlights come my way. I moved to the middle of that road and waved my arms. Please, God, I prayed, let him stop, at least don't let him hit me.

The beat up Chevy pickup stopped, and the driver, a young guy, rolled down the passenger side window. When he asked if I needed help, I told him the deer hit me, and I needed a ride to civilization.

"No worries, I'm going to Philly," he said, like he already knew where I was going. I climbed in, happier than when I won six hundred bucks at the Atlantic City slots.

The kid looked early twenties. Hippie type, long hair, scruffy beard, but a really soft voice, the kind that goes up at the end of a sentence. I hoped he wasn't on drugs, but God Almighty, I'd of gotten in the car with Tony Soprano to get off that road.

Before he started driving, he stared at me, and said real nice, "You're bloody. You need to go to the hospital?"

"Nah, I'm okay," I told him, and asked to use his cell phone. I thought I should call Bill and tell him what happened. I got no one else to call. My wife, ex-wife, moved to Rhode Island when her boss transferred there. She did not go for her job. Screw her anyway. The son is in graduate school in Memphis, still a Mama's boy, and we don't talk much. He lives his life, I live mine, and that works for us. So it's pretty much just me, living in the row house my parents left me, fending for myself. I do okay. I got friends from the transit agency, and friends from the neighborhood, people I've known all my life. But no one to report to. That's what I call freedom.

So the kid says, "I don't have a cell phone."

"I thought all you kids had cell phones, iPods, the works," I said.

"I don't need one. My housemates would let me use their phones if I had to make a call, but I never do." He sounded nonchalant.

"Where you from? Why're you driving through the Pine Barrens in the middle of a Sunday night?" I asked.

"The guys I share a house with near LaSalle were having a Halloween party tonight, so I left and drove to the shore. I love the ocean, especially when beaches are empty. It was nice today, quiet. I thought about staying and sleeping on the sand, but you called me. People are always calling me. It makes it hard to think."

So I'm thinking, *Twilight Zone,* and watching for street signs to make sure I'm right here on *terra firma*, you know what I'm saying? But I had to talk to the guy.

"I don't remember calling you, but I'm glad you came," I said, and he said, "I know."

The truck bounced along the bumpy road. Its headlights hardly cut through the haze. I couldn't see much except the fuzzy headlight glow until we reached Route 30 and streetlights.

I was never so glad to see a clerk through Wawa's plate glass window, or price signs high above closed gas stations. Tell you the truth, I'd been worried about ever getting off that road. I touched my forehead. The cut above my eyebrow felt sticky and slimy, like fish gills. The guy glanced over and raised his eyebrows.

"You got it bleeding again." He fumbled in his pocket for a hanky.

I know, what kid carries a hanky? He gave it to me and told me to apply direct pressure, so I did. Damn, it hurt, but it was nice of the kid, so I thought I should talk to him.

"You go to LaSalle?" I said.

"Supposedly. I hoped it would work out, but I haven't made it through any classes. I have a hard time sitting still, listening to the stupid crap people say. I just can't focus. It seems so . . ." He stopped mid-sentence.

The car was real quiet. He turned off Route 30 onto 73. At least we were going in the right direction. I got to tell you, by then I was pretty woozy. I leaned my head back and closed my eyes. I almost fell asleep but he started talking again.

"I write poetry, so my major's English, you know?"

I shook my head to wake up. "Yeah, sounds great. Lots of good poetry jobs waiting out there. But you got to go to class, right? You got to ignore the stupid stuff, and pay attention to the important stuff."

"I try," he said, "but I think about everything. My mother says I think too much. It's a funny thing, you know? Lots of people go their whole lives without thinking at all. They're the lucky ones. I can't stop thinking. I can't stop hearing. Always, someone's calling me, needing me. It doesn't stop. I can't make it stop."

So, I said, "Man, I'm one of the lucky ones. The only thinking I do is about what to have for dinner. You should appreciate the opportunity to go to college. I never had the chance. My old man couldn't wait for me to get a job, and be a man. It's too late for me, but you're young. This is your time. You should get the most out of it, enjoy it, because it's damned hard to go back."

He stared straight ahead. "This is my going back."

"To LaSalle?" I asked. He didn't look old enough to be in his second career or anything.

"I always wanted to be a pilot. My grandfather was a Navy pilot in World War II. I loved him and wanted to be like him. I actually got into an aviation school in Florida where you study for your college degree and pilot's license at the same time," he said.

"That sounds good," I said. "So what happened with that?"

Al's Auto Repair, Johnny's Tap Room, Vito's Deli, Hair Today, an Acme supermarket, and Beverly's Bakery passed by like we were in an old moving picture. I figured he didn't hear my question, or didn't like it. I touched my eyebrow. It stopped bleeding. Finally, he answered.

"I was eighteen when I went to Florida. Paul, my roommate, was twenty-five. We shared an apartment near the airport. We registered for flight training, and I signed up for Math and English. At first, it was good, but after a few weeks, Paul took over my brain, you know? And other people kept calling me, telling me things. They knew where I lived. I couldn't leave my room. Then, Paul called my mother. She drove all the way to Florida to bring me to a hospital in Philly. When I came home from the hospital, she said since I was feeling better, I should think about college. It seemed like a good idea."

The kid rubbed his finger along the side of his nose. He started taking short tight breaths, and I got to tell you, I was freaking out.

So I said, real quiet, "Son, you OK? I appreciate the ride, you have no idea how much, but you're making me nervous. No offense, but I never met a guy like you. You're different."

"Yeah, no offense." His laugh was bitter. "Do you know how many people tell me I'm different? In high school, I was never invited to parties, to hang out, whatever. I was on the cross-country team and won the district championship. Even so, they laughed at me, and called me creepy. Just that one girl, Caitlyn, talked to me. She said being different isn't bad, but it's hard, because I feel things more deeply than other people. She told me I have a poet's soul. Caitlyn's my only friend. Since she goes to LaSalle, I figured that's where I'd go. I saw her in the library a couple times but didn't talk to her. There were too many people around."

A girl. That made sense. Believe me, I was pretty sure the kid was on something, but I wasn't afraid. He seemed gentle, just, you know, troubled. Maybe I'm stupid or maybe I'm nuts, but I liked the guy, even though I had no idea what the hell he was talking about.

So I just said, "Yeah, that's tough."

Then he said, "Do you know about Maya, the circle of illusion? When I walk through the city nothing's real. Everything's make-believe. All people care about is money. But money's only numbers on paper. Why fight and kill over pieces of paper? Do you ever ask yourself what life is about? Why we're here? Why are you and I, strangers, riding in my truck at this instant, on this road? Why do we get up every day, go to school, go to work, go home, start again? See what I mean? It's a circle. My father worked in a bank for twenty-five years. The year he retired, he died from a heart attack. What happened to the person he was, or the space he took up? Where did he go? The only real thing is death."

We were getting close to the Tacony Palmyra Bridge. Toll booths took shape under the glow of lights flickering over the drawbridge span. I dug out four bloody dollars from my pocket for the toll. After he paid the toll taker, he started to drive through, but jammed on the brakes, and rummaged through his pockets. What the hell, I'm thinking, we already paid. He hopped out, ran to the booth, then raced back. I got to tell you, it was disturbing,

When he slid into his seat, he said, "The woman behind us didn't have any money."

I'm wondering how he could know that, and he tells me.

"People call me, all the time. That's how I found you."

We crossed the bridge and drove west on Levick Street. It must have been midnight. The streetlights glowed hazy and yellow. Behind venetian blinds in rowhouses on both sides of the street, shadows moved about their business. Skeletons, witches, and black cats bounced in tiny front yards decorated for Halloween.

"Do you know Rimbaud?" he asked.

"Rambo? Sure. I like Rocky better. More realistic, you know? I love Stallone." Finally, he was beginning to talk sense.

When he turned to look at me, his eyes were squinty. He didn't say anything for a couple seconds, then he began to laugh, like when you're a kid in church, and the nuns are glaring, and you know you have to stop but can't, and you laugh even harder. I started laughing too. Tears rolled down my face.

I was afraid he'd plow into a parked car, but he got serious.

"Rocky is definitely the better movie," he agreed. "But I didn't say Rambo, I said, *Rimbaud.* You know, the French poet who died when he was like 35."

"Never heard of him," I said. It sounded like Rambo to me.

"The guy did his best work by the time he was 20, then took off to Africa and never wrote again. He wrote this book of poems called, *Season in Hell.* The first time I read it, I felt like, he gets it, you know?"

City streetlights shone through the windshield and I got a good look at the kid's face. Brown hair and beard, green eyes glazed like he had a fever. I swear, I thought he had tears in his eyes. The weird thing was, I started to think like him. I wondered why I was on that road in New Jersey at the exact time the deer decided to crash into a car, and why this pilot-poet-circle-of-illusion guy came by to give me a lift.

When we turned onto Roosevelt Boulevard, I felt more like myself. Thank God, my house was only fifteen minutes away.

He starting talking again, and it took a moment to realize he was quoting a poem.

. . .One evening I took Beauty in my arms - and I thought her bitter - and I insulted her. I steeled myself against justice. I fled. O witches, O misery, O hate, my treasure was left in your care! I have withered within me all human hope. With the silent leap of a sullen beast, I have downed and strangled every joy . . .

"Rimbaud," he said.

"Frankly, I'll take Rambo – less violent," I said.

We started laughing again, crazy laughing.

When we turned onto Germantown Avenue, I told him, "I live on West Mount Airy."

"Down by the Allen Lane Station?" he said.

I asked how he knew that.

"I know the area," he said.

We got a parking space close to my house.

"You wanna come in, get something to eat?" I thought I should be polite, him driving me all that way.

"No, thanks," he said. "You OK?"

"Sure," I said. "Thanks for the ride."

I opened the door but when I tried to get out, I got real dizzy, and fell back against the seat.

"I'll help you in," he said.

I didn't even pretend I didn't need help. Man, I was never so happy to walk through my front door. The mail was jammed up in the slot, and the house smelled like old socks and tuna fish.

"I'll boil water for tea," I said.

My mother made tea when I was sick or upset, so it seemed the thing to do. I guess my knees collapsed, because I passed out cold between the dining room and the kitchen. Next thing I know, I'm flat on my back looking up into his eyes.

"Whoa there, buddy, I better call 9-1-1," he said. His eyes flitted around the room, looking for a phone I guess.

"No, don't, I don't want all those bells, and sirens, and lights. I'll be OK. It's been a long night," I said.

He helped me sit in a dining room chair, then wet a dishrag that wasn't too dirty, and wiped blood off my face. The cut started bleeding again. I didn't have bandages or gauze in the house, so he went upstairs and found an old undershirt. When he wrapped it around my head, he called it, my *red badge of courage.*

He must have helped me upstairs, because I woke up in my bed with the phone ringing, and the sun in my eyes. Throbbing headache, holy God almighty, every muscle in my body ached. It took all my strength to grab the phone on the nightstand. It was Joyce, our dispatcher, asking where I was. I told her about the accident and promised I'd be in tomorrow.

My left eye was swollen shut and looked purple in the mirror. I unwound the bloody undershirt from my head. It was crusted brown, and smelled like death. I got myself into the bathtub and turned on the water, hot as I could stand. I thought about last night, and heard his voice — *I have withered within me all human hope.*

After the bath, I felt better. With the crusty blood washed away, the thick slash on my forehead oozed just a little. Probably needed stitches. It'll leave a nice scar. I'll look like Rocky. I found some Bayer in the medicine cabinet and chewed a handful, then went downstairs. I made coffee, hot and strong, and poured it in my father's cracked cup.

In the living room, I shoved a bunch of magazines and bills off the end table to make room for the cup. That was when I saw it. On the cover of a small, dog-eared book, a naked man spread his arms like he was hanging on a cross. Across the top, orange letters spelled, *A Season in Hell* by Arthur Rimbaud.

I sipped coffee and looked for the guy's name and address inside the book. Nothing. I flipped through the pages until I found *A Season in Hell*, the poem the kid quoted. Then I read *The Drunken Boat* because I figured it was like me yesterday, drunk on the fishing boat. But it wasn't. The last few stanzas were underlined. I read them out loud.

> *But, truly, I have wept too much! The Dawns are heartbreaking. Every moon is atrocious and every sun bitter: Sharp love has swollen me up with heady langours. O let my keel split! O let me sink to the bottom! If there is one water in Europe I want, it is the Black cold pool where into the scented twilight A child squatting full of sadness, launches A boat as fragile as a butterfly in May. I can no more, bathed in your langours, O waves, Sail in the wake of the carriers of cottons, Nor undergo the pride of the flags and pennants, Nor pull past the horrible eyes of the hulks.*

The words were pretty but bizarre. They floated in the room then disappeared, out of place in this house. I wondered why I was reading that poem at that minute? I read the poem again - *I can no more.*

I wanted to talk to the kid to figure out what Rimbaud meant when he wrote these poems. *Every moon is atrocious and every sun bitter.* Talk about what's real and what's an illusion!

Since my wrecked car was stuck in the Pine Barrens of New Jersey, I figured I'd take the bus to LaSalle, check the library, and search campus until I found him. I'd return his book, and invite him to dinner to thank him for the ride. I didn't even know his name.

I swirled the coffee around the cup until tiny drops seeped through the crack in the porcelain. I must have dozed off. When I woke up, my stomach felt like an erupting volcano. Coffee with aspirin wasn't a great idea. I found a box of saltines in the pantry and spread them with Velveeta. I filled a glass with faucet water — the old Philly chemical cocktail. After I ate, my stomach felt better.

I figured I better call my car insurance company and start looking at used car ads. But first, I turned on the TV while I thumbed through the kid's poetry book.

I half-listened to Action News until the traffic report drew my attention — an early morning vehicle fire near LaSalle University.

Traffic is at a standstill. Your best bet is to avoid this area. We have Erin on the scene. Just look at the smoke and cinders floating behind her. What can you tell us, Erin?

As you can see, behind me is the smoldering frame of the Chevy pickup that crashed into this utility pole. Before the debris is hauled away and the road opened, the accident reconstruction crew needs to complete its investigation. It appears the driver was the only occupant of this single vehicle crash. Moms, you might want to send the kids to another room before I continue. This was an inferno. The driver was burned beyond recognition, and at this time, police have no information about the driver's identity. Even the license plate was incinerated. They're trying to determine what caused the crash and the fiery aftermath. Police ask anyone who witnessed this crash or recognize this badly burned vehicle to call the information hotline at 215-222-5555. This is Erin O'Malley on the scene of the early morning crash and fire that caused today's traffic nightmare.

No, God, no. It isn't him. It can't be him.

8

MUSCLE TOWN

E van was a small man with strawberry-blond hair and watery blue eyes magnified by wire-rimmed glasses. He wore expensive suits, crisp white shirts, and Italian ties. At twenty-seven, with MBA and CPA after his name, he considered himself quite a catch. By living with his parents, he'd invested most of his salary, and the value of his investment portfolio was substantial. His parents, however, despaired of the preppy conservative fellow who entered the world through their flower-child loins. *Peace, love, and rock and roll* was their motto. Evan was a Republican.

Alone in the elevator car, Evan raised his chin to straighten his tie while the luminescent green number changed from 1 to 2 to 3 to 4 to 5. When the doors slid open, he stepped into the hallway, turned right, and paused outside the door to Astral Projections, the small investment firm where he'd worked happily these past three years. He imagined his name — Evan Jennings, CFO — stenciled on the plate-glass door. In a few years, his uncle Bill — who owned the company and had no children — would retire, and Evan was heir apparent — until Bill hired Jimmy Boyd.

Like Evan's parents, Bill remained faithful to his hippie roots. He wore suits as an act of surrender, and tied his long grey hair in a ponytail — an affectation Evan found antiquated if harmless. Not harmless, in Evan's opinion, was Bill's obsession with fitness. On Evan's first day at Astral Projections, Bill insisted he run with him along East River Drive and later, lift weights in the basement gym. After that first week, whenever he heard Bill's footsteps, Evan took out his inhaler. Now, Jimmy Boyd ran and lifted weights with Bill.

Each time Evan thought about the random way Bill hired Jimmy, who wouldn't even have a college degree until December after he presented his senior project, his hands knotted in fists, and his jaw clenched.

Three months ago, on a Sunday in June, the Phillies played the Nationals in a double header. By happenstance, Jimmy Boyd's seat at the ballpark was next to Bill. The next morning, Evan stepped out of the elevator to find a muscular young guy in casual clothes waiting outside Astral Projections' door.

"Dude, you work here?" Jimmy asked.

Evan nodded and unlocked the door. Before he entered the office, the elevator door opened. Bill stepped out, shouted, "Jimbo! you found us," slung his arm across Jimmy's shoulders, and ushered him into Astral Projections, leaving Evan speechless in the hallway. Without an application or formal interview, Jimmy Boyd became the new Astral Projections analyst, with a windowed office next to Evan.

Today, as the glass doors swished shut behind him, Evan greeted Judy at the reception desk with a pleasant, "Good morning." She responded with a distracted wave.

Jimmy, wearing a yellow polo shirt and khakis, knelt beside her, admiring photos from her family trip to Disney World. As Evan rounded the corner to his office, he heard them laughing. He knew they were laughing at him.

After he flicked on his computer, he sipped tea from a black porcelain cup printed with the company logo, a spectral body floating over the Earth. Bill loved the image. When Evan became CFO, he'd change the logo to the initials AP inside a triangle, with sharp lines and tidy edges. Only the smartest people, like Susan, would keep their jobs. Jimmy Boyd would definitely go.

In her office across the hall, Susan shuffled files and slammed a drawer. Although she wasn't a beautiful woman, Susan was intelligent and capable. Evan admired her efficiency, a quality he attributed to her maturity — she was in her mid-thirties. Her recent divorce added to her appeal, and Evan felt confident they were headed for a relationship. Susan sat beside him at meetings, and they often had lunch together. As soon as the time was right, he planned to ask her on a date.

When his door burst open and slammed the wall, Evan dropped his cup. Hot tea spattered across his lap and seeped through his slacks. Jimmy Boyd entered as if he were welcome, and sat in the guest chair. Evan dabbed his legs with a tissue, and glanced at the clock. Until Nordstrom opened at 10:00, he'd suffer with wet pants and chafing thighs. He narrowed his eyes.

"Whassup?" Jimmy said in his grating voice.

"What's up is, I'm working." Evan stood and brushed his pants.

"Whoa, Dude, wet your pants?" Jimmy asked, upper lip curled in a smirk.

Evan bristled. "No, Jimmy, I didn't wet my pants. When you slammed the door, my tea spilled." The nerve of this guy, Evan thought, shaking his head.

"Tea's so girly." Jimmy finally noticed Evan's angry stare. "Hey, don't mind me. What do I know, right?"

"Right," Evan said. He examined the seat of his chair and dried it with a clump of tissues before sitting down again. "Did you want something, Jimmy?"

Jimmy tilted his head and flashed his winning smile. Evan swallowed. The smile made Evan think the guy actually liked him, but he refused to be taken in by his phony charm.

"Bro, Bill says talk to you, you pull in the big bucks around here. Me, I got bills to pay, and I'm running through savings like water. You got any business to throw my way?"

"I'll tell Judy to send you the blind calls."

"Blind calls ain't gonna cut it. I don't have rich parents like you to put me through college and send their rich friends to invest with me," Jimmy said, eyes sad.

A government analyst and a public school teacher didn't represent rich parents in Evan's mind. So what if the white-bread middle-class families that kept him in Armani suits happened to be his parents' friends?

"Why don't you sell life insurance to your buddies? Or get them to invest fifty a month in our mutual fund? Everyone has contacts, it's what you do with them that matters," Evan said in what he hoped was a sarcastic voice.

"Those boys don't give a crap about insurance or investing." Jimmy shook his head. "Old people are the ones with money. I've been thinking about how to get their business, and got an idea. I'm going to offer free retirement planning seminars at the library. Judy reserved a room, and Susan approved petty cash for coffee and donuts."

Evan forced a smile. "Good luck with that."

Old people aren't going to listen to retirement advice from Jimmy Boyd. Good manners kept him from laughing.

Jimmy pushed back his chair. "Bill's got a bunch of meetings in New York the next couple days. He said to tell you to spot me in the gym after work." He flexed his right arm where a ship sailed on blue waves in a sea lane of veins. "We'll work on your scrawny bod, too."

"I don't have gym clothes," Evan said, flabbergasted.

"Get your ass down there at 4:30. You'll be home to Mommy by 6:00." Jimmy slammed the door when he left.

Evan bit his lip. Now, when he went to Nordstrom for new pants, he'd have to buy gym shorts, socks, a T-shirt for God's sake, and sneakers. And he did not appreciate the Mommy crack. Darn Bill for tricking him into going to the gym. Ever since that summer at band camp when he broke his glasses in the swirly episode, Evan avoided guys like Jimmy. Why didn't Bill tell him about the New York trip?

Evan's phone rang. After he exchanged pleasantries with Mrs. Kenney, the principal at his mother's elementary school, he pulled up her account.

"Since you plan to retire in five years, let's keep your money safe. I recommend we ladder your retirement savings in six month, nine month, and twelve month CDs. Once the market settles, we'll find safe, higher-yielding investments."

Muffled talk and Jimmy's laughter came from Susan's office. Evan's hands trembled. His cheeks burned.

"Right, three CDs for $80K each to ensure FDIC coverage. I'm afraid I have to cut this short, Mrs. Kenney. Say hello to Mr. Kenney for me."

He hung up quietly, tiptoed across his office, and pressed his ear to the door. His heart raced, and he clenched his fists at the sound of soft voices, grunts, and rhythmic thumping.

He threw open his door and rushed into Susan's office, shouting, "Stop!"

Susan's hand was at her throat. Jimmy squatted below her. They stared at him wide-eyed.

"What the hell, Evan!" Jimmy said.

"Stop what? The noise?" Susan asked. "Sorry. My file drawer jammed and I asked Jimmy to open it. I didn't realize we'd disturb you."

The drawer screeched open.

"Got it," Jimmy said. "There's the culprit." He tossed an overstuffed folder on the desk. "After we get back from lunch, I'll spray WD40 on the runners."

He pushed past Evan and muttered, "Dude."

Evan slid into the guest chair, still warm from Jimmy's thighs.

Susan stopped shuffling papers. "What do you need, Evan?" she asked in her I'm busy voice.

Her dark wavy hair kissed her collar, and bangs feathered her forehead. Her deep brown eyes peered out over high cheekbones and a Roman nose.

"Just being friendly." Evan plucked at his slacks, worried he'd leave a wet spot on the chair. "Is that last quarter's results?"

"Yes. Bill will be pleased. Jimmy's numbers get better each month." Susan's even white teeth gleamed.

"Great. My advice is paying off. After work, I'm going down to work out, and Jimmy needs me to spot him on the equipment," he said with a confident smile.

"I love when he flexes his muscles. Jimmy's got it all — brains and brawn." Susan's giggle made Evan feel dirty.

"I think it's creepy, showing off muscles all the time."

Susan wrinkled her nose. "Jimmy's anything but creepy."

"Sure. Whatever. Got to get back to the grind."

Evan never expected Susan to fall for the muscle boy thing, and he didn't realize Jimmy's numbers were improving each month. He pushed away the nagging thought that Jimmy's retirement planning meetings might be a good idea.

PROMPTLY AT 4:30, Evan fastidiously hung his shirt and suit in a locker. He changed into the compression briefs, fast-dry shirt and shorts, black low-cut socks, and Adidas sneakers his Nordstrom personal shopper assured him were essential. Added to the cost of new slacks and underwear, he'd blown three hundred bucks. He pushed back his glasses and entered the gym.

Cybex machines lined the room's right side, while stacks of free weights were arranged along the left. In the mirrored walls, a dozen Evans cleaned their glasses, then stepped on treadmills.

After he studied the console, he set the control to 3.6 mph with a 2% incline. As he walked, Evan decided in a few days, maybe next week, he'd ask Susan to stay late to help with a project. After everyone left, he'd enter her office.

She'd ask, "Why did you shut the door, Evan?"

"I thought we needed privacy," he'd say, a soulful look in his eyes.

She'd blush and say, "Oh, Evan, I've been dreaming of this."

He'd approach slowly, kneel, take her hands, and gaze into eyes filled with longing. They'd . . .

"Dude, I've been standing here for like five minutes. Cute outfit. Your mom pick it out? You could wear heels with those legs."

Jimmy stood, arms folded, head tipped. Evan blushed. He glanced down, grateful for the costly compression briefs. Beads of sweat dotted his forehead. He stepped off the treadmill and dabbed his face with a towel.

Jimmy's scent, of sweat and musk, emanated from deltoids bulging under a grey sleeveless shirt that outlined his firm nipples. Thick blue veins wrapped his biceps and triceps, flowed to his wrists, and across the tops of his hands. His baggy shorts hugged his rounded glutes, and his calves looked like fists.

When he saw Evan studying him, Jimmy planted his right foot and moved his left leg forward, toes pointed down.

"Nice, right? This body, my friend, is a contender for the Pennsylvania All-Natural Bodybuilding Championship." He lifted his shirt. Four rectangles ran along each side of a taut perpendicular line. "These are called abs, Son."

Evan's mouth filled with saliva. He thought of the strong boys at band camp who held him upside down and dunked his head in the toilet.

"If I'm gonna make you a babe magnet, we gotta stick to a schedule." Jimmy tapped a memo book. "Got our workout right here. First we'll stretch the hammies."

"I only came today because Bill's in New York," Evan said.

Jimmy spread a mat on the floor, and lay on his back with one leg in the air. "Bill gave me a direct order — get Evan to the gym. And there's the safety issue. I can't lift without a spotter, and I have to lift to win that contest. Besides, dudes hang with dudes, right?"

Evan bit his lower lip, pulled off his glasses, and cleaned them. Where did the terms of employment require fitness sessions with Arnold Schwarzenegger?

Jimmy stretched his other leg. "Brother, those nerdy glasses will fog up every time we work out. Ever hear of laser surgery? Do it, man. Now get a mat. We're doing crunches. Exhale up, inhale down."

Each time Evan strained for a sit-up, he studied Jimmy's incline board crunches. Finally, Jimmy rolled off the board. Evan stood, too. He tightened his stomach, expecting a punch, but Jimmy moved to the mirrors.

"Squats are your most important exercise. Watch. Weight goes on the heels. Keep your knees above your toes. After squats, we'll do lunges."

Jimmy demonstrated each move and, when Evan tried, corrected his form.

After what seemed like hundreds of squats and lunges, Evan's quads burned, his glutes cramped, his knees ached, and he wanted to go home. Instead, Jimmy maneuvered him to the bench press. He grabbed two forty-five-pound plates, slid them on the bar, then added forty-five pounds to each side, and lay down on the bench.

"The bar weighs forty pounds. With one-eighty in plates, I got two-twenty total." Jimmy shook his shoulders. He filled his lungs then exhaled. Then he unracked the bar and raised it. He inhaled each time he lowered the bar and exhaled each time he pressed up. Up and down, breathe out, breathe in, breathe out. After twelve presses, Jimmy dropped the bar on the rack. It sounded like a skull cracking.

"I really should get going." Evan's new shorts felt as clammy as his tea-spattered slacks had. His insides quivered. He hoped Jimmy couldn't tell.

"You got one more station, Dude."

Jimmy led Evan to a big metal contraption that looked like a cage, and he knew he was trapped.

"This is a Smith machine. It's easier to bench press because the tracks stabilize the bar. Lie on the bench and grab the bar."

Standing so close, Jimmy's smell — skunky and warm — filled Evan's nostrils. Jimmy moved Evan's hands to mid-grip, and he wondered what the hell he was doing here. But after he did sixteen reps, he felt strong and proud.

"You got the motion. Try it with weight this time," Jimmy said. "Twenty pounds to start."

Evan took a breath, gripped the bar, and exhaled to press up, but the bar didn't move. He inhaled, then exhaled and pushed. His pecs and biceps trembled, but the bar barely moved. Jimmy loomed over him with a crooked smile, raised the bar, and hooked it in place.

When Evan got to his feet, he felt weak-kneed and exhausted. He moved toward the locker room.

"We lift Mondays, Wednesdays, and Fridays. Tuesdays and Thursdays we run. You need to build up your bod, Evan. Stop at Muscle Town, get a big tub of protein powder, and make yourself a shake as soon as you get home. Protein, Dude, protein."

When Jimmy twirled his towel into a rope, Evan flinched. Jimmy curled his upper lip and flicked the towel around his neck.

"You think I'd towel whip you? That's lame, Bro."

In the locker room, Evan wondered about the symptoms of a heart attack. He changed into his suit, stuck his tie in his pocket, and grabbed his briefcase. When he rushed out the locker room door, Bill was leaning against a wall, sweat curling his ponytail and darkening his Astral Projections T-shirt.

"About time you started lifting, Evan. You'll get addicted, right, Jimbo?" Bill said.

"Right, Boss Man."

"I thought you went to New York." Evan flinched at the whine in his voice.

"Tomorrow."

Jimmy stood by the free weights, preparing to lift giant dumbbells over his head. "Boss, when you gonna retire that hippie hairdo?"

As Evan crept to the door, Bill crossed the room to spot Jimmy.

AT MUSCLE TOWN, Evan shelled out fifty bucks for protein powder and energy bars. When he got home, he was too sore and tired to make a shake. Instead, he toyed with the tofu fried rice his mother made, and went to bed early. At 2:00 a.m., he woke to terrible leg cramps. He filled the tub with hot water and soaked until his alarm went off at 7:00. His arms were so sore his dad buttoned his shirt and tied his tie.

EVAN SIPPED green tea at his desk, called his clients, checked the markets, and made an appointment for laser eye surgery. When he heard Jimmy and Susan laughing, he didn't care. He counted the hours until he could go home and sit on a heating pad.

THE DAY AFTER *LASIK* SURGERY, Evan deposited his spectacles in the Lions Club box. He got his hair cut tight on the sides and spiky on top.

Mondays, Wednesdays, and Fridays, he headed to the gym at 4:30. On Tuesdays and Thursdays, he and Jimmy ran along East River Drive during lunch hour. In six weeks, he gained eight pounds — pounds of manly muscle, Jimmy said.

When he looked in the mirror, Evan liked what he saw. At night — behind a locked door after his mother barged in with his laundry — he posed in his jockey shorts. When he flexed, his biceps popped.

ON A TUESDAY MORNING IN NOVEMBER, when Evan heard voices in the conference room, he knocked on the door.

"We're busy in here," Bill said. "It better be important."

Before he retreated, Bill opened the door. "Oh, Evan, come in. Jimmy's practicing his senior presentation. I think you'll find it impressive."

Evan swallowed, straightened his tie, and took a chair.

"I'll start over," Jimmy said. "Each time I held retirement planning seminars at the library, all sorts of people, not just senior citizens, came into the meeting room. I thought they just wanted free coffee, but when they stayed, I realized everybody needs money help, and nobody knows where to find it. I decided to make my senior project a slide show to educate financial advisors how to reach people — young, old, middle-aged, black, white, yellow, brown, whatever — to help them manage their money."

A lump formed in Evan's throat. He should have paid more attention when Jimmy talked about his retirement planning meetings. Since he offered them free, they seemed like a ton of work for nothing. Now, he felt ambushed, like the rules changed but no one told him.

Despite the cloying smell of Bill's hazelnut coffee and stale conference room air, when Jimmy's first PowerPoint image hit the screen, Evan became focused and amazed.

The Astral Projections logo of a phantasmal body floating over the Earth transmogrified like a kaleidoscope into a Hispanic woman in a pink sweatshirt, who turned into an ancient Asian man in a wheelchair, a white mother with a toddler in arms, a middle-aged married couple, a young black man, a white-haired woman with a cane, and two thirty-something men holding hands. The next frame showed these same people sitting with Jimmy around a conference table. In the background, the song, *The Happening,* played. Before his eyes, the people transformed into cartoon characters, disturbingly true to their photographic images.

Each slide showed a different cartoon person or couple with cartoon Jimmy, who pointed to a white board listing issues, risk tolerances, and investment goals for that specific demographic, while a popular song captured the essence of the target group. In the slide where cartoon Jimmy and cartoon young black man considered his financial goals — university education, a good job, a nice house —John Legend sang *Wake Up Everybody,* in the background.

"Brilliant," Bill murmured.

On the last slide, cartoon people and cartoon Jimmy danced to Pink's *Get The Party Started*, then transmogrified to real people dancing. Along the slide's bottom, a message flashed: *Dance with me.*

When Jimmy flipped off the projector, he grinned with relief. Bill clapped and cheered, "Bravo. A triumph! That's how you blend the cosmic with the temporal. People identify with songs from their era. Shows you understand where they come from."

"Nice effects," Evan said.

"Thanks, Dude." Jimmy smiled in his disarming way. "I need a favor. Bill asked me to present the slide show at his Investment Managers meeting. I need to a nice suit and stuff, but I don't have a clue what to get or where to shop. Bill says you're the man to help me dress for success."

With Bill's hand on his shoulder, Jimmy looked like a shy high school boy. Evan narrowed his laser-flat eyes. Before he came up with an excuse, Bill pulled out his wallet and handed Evan a bank card.

"You boys get lunch on me then go shopping. This slide show will create a new business for us — outreach and training." Bill flicked his ponytail. "Today a new era dawns at Astral Projections. Evan's sporting a new look, and Jimmy soon will be. I think it's time I enter the 21st century. After work, Jimbo, you can lop off my ponytail. *It's gettin' kind a long."*

As Evan stepped to the door, Jimmy called, "12:30, right?"

"Right," Evan answered, but he no longer knew what was right. He pressed the bridge of his nose where his glasses used to be.

AFTER LUNCH, they met his Nordstrom personal shopper, and Evan felt more confident.

"Show us mid-weight wools — blues and greys. Something he can wear to the office, the boardroom, or the opera."

Jimmy rolled his eyes.

After the personal shopper sized Jimmy, he brought three shirts and six suits to the dressing room. Evan decided on charcoal grey suit with a two-button jacket for Jimmy. As the tailor scooted around for measurements, Jimmy posed like an uncomfortable teenager.

At the shoe department, Evan recommended black wing tips, and added three pairs of dark Egyptian-cotton socks. When Jimmy saw the belt prices — some cost more than $300 — he gasped, but Evan found a nice leather belt on the clearance rack.

Jimmy chose a blue-and-red-striped tie. Evan selected one with a blue paisley design and paid for it with his own cash. When he presented it to Jimmy, he blushed and thanked him.

After they returned to work, Evan handed Bill the receipts. He didn't bat an eye.

AT THE END of the day, everyone gathered in the conference room. Bill stripped to his undershirt, and Judy played *Almost Cut My Hair* on her laptop.

"Let's do it," Bill said.

Bill's hair was so thick, Jimmy sawed at the ponytail but couldn't lop it off. Susan took the scissors, and cut Bill's hair into tight grey curls. After the floor was covered with hair, she handed Bill a mirror.

He turned his head from side to side and announced, "I look like Will Ferrell."

THE CHRISTMAS CONCERT tickets arrived the day after Thanksgiving. In front of his bedroom mirror, Evan practiced asking Susan for a date.

"Will you honor me with your presence at the concert next weekend?" He pulled the tickets from his shirt pocket and offered them with a bow and a sweet smile. He couldn't wait to surprise her.

Monday morning, Evan's hands trembled while he waited outside Susan's office until she waved him in.

"You're looking good," Susan said.

"I'm just a sexy boy." Evan flexed.

Susan smiled. "And you think you're cute. Really, though, Jimmy's nice to train you, with everything he's got going — preparing for college graduation, racking up sales, and next weekend he's competing in the All Natural Bodybuilding Championship in York. He invited me to come. Here's his application photo."

Evan studied the picture. Bronze Jimmy in a blue thong just crushed Evan's plan to wine and dine Susan. Jimmy's muscles bulged as if rendered by Michelangelo. He looked like a god — an Atlas Evan condemned to carry the world for eternity.

"He's practically naked. It's vulgar." Evan couldn't stop himself.

Susan slid a spreadsheet across the desk. "There's nothing vulgar about that body. And look at this revenue."

Money was flowing in from the new training program called, *Dance With Me,* based on Jimmy's slide show and a binder of investment options.

The concert tickets pressed against Evan's chest like a brick.

THAT AFTERNOON as Evan ran on the treadmill, he felt reckless. He decided to confront Jimmy about Susan. He picked up his pace, and didn't hear Jimmy come in.

"Brother, keep running like that, you're gonna spring the belt," Jimmy said. "Impressive, but you still got girly legs."

Sweating and panting, Evan slowed the machine and hopped off.

Everything about Jimmy infuriated him — the beanie pulled down to his eyebrows, the black tank shirt that accentuated his pecs, his orange mesh shorts, his lopsided smile. Fists clenched and cheeks flushed, Evan faced Jimmy.

"What's up your butt?" Jimmy asked, brow furrowed.

"Are you taking Susan to your bodybuilding thing next weekend?"

"She asked if she could come. I like her. She's good company."

Jimmy folded his arms and narrowed his eyes. An outdoors smell diluted his natural skunky odor.

"You know I've been waiting until she got over her divorce to ask her out. I didn't want to rush her, a courtesy that's beyond you, apparently."

Evan threw down his towel, picked it up, wiped his neck, and moved to the lat machine.

"What're you saying, Bro? You didn't tell me you had a thing with her, and she never said anything about you."

Jimmy set the lat pin for Evan to eighty pounds. Evan grasped the bar and pulled it to his chest. He eased the bar back up.

"Ninety pounds," Evan said. "Look, Bro, I spent three hundred dollars on tickets to the orchestra for next weekend. Then, when I'm about to surprise her, she shoves a picture at me of you practically naked, and swoons about going to the competition with you. After all I've done for you." As soon as he said it, he wished he hadn't. "Move it to a hundred."

Jimmy adjusted the weight deck. He stared in the mirror while Evan pulled down the bar and let it rise.

When Evan moved to the cable machine and started on triceps, Jimmy stayed where he was, staring.

Eventually, Jimmy, face hard, joined Evan at the bicep machine.

"OK," Jimmy said.

"OK what?" Evan puffed.

"I'll tell Susan I'm meeting a girlfriend in York. I'll tell her it's not a good time."

"Why would you do that?"

"The last thing I need is a relationship hassle. You're more her type anyway — professional, polite. I'm just a grunt trying to make something of myself."

Evan started toward the locker room but stopped. "You need me to spot you?"

"Nah. I'm done. I gotta pick up my suit at Nordstrom. Wanna come?"

More than anything, Evan wanted to go with Jimmy, see him in his new suit, adjust the shoulders, nod when the jacket fell perfectly across his broad chest, and accept Jimmy's compliments about his fashion sense. But he felt empty.

With every heartbeat, he'd prepared for Jimmy's disdain — *Dude, you think that fine woman would rather go to the orchestra with you than smear oil all over my body and scream my name when I cross the stage?* Instead, Jimmy's easy surrender left him deflated and depressed. He worried about Susan's feelings. Would she consider Evan the knight in shining armor protecting her honor with his invitation to the concert? Or would she see him as a pitiful poser with laser eyes, trendy hair, a stuffy suit, and pompous ways? Evan didn't make Susan feel pretty and young, but Jimmy did. Still, he couldn't stomach her going to York with Jimmy.

"You coming or not?" Jimmy called, twirling his towel.

"I guess."

Jimmy snapped his butt, and Evan yelled, "Hey!"

AT 4:00 on a snowy January day, after everyone rushed home to avoid the icy streets, Evan took the elevator to the basement gym. He ran thirty minutes on the treadmill before going to the Smith machine for chest presses. He slid forty-five-pound plates on each side of the bar, settled on the bench, and shook his shoulders. He took a deep breath, grabbed the bar, exhaled, and pressed. Too easy. He added forty-five pounds to each side. Cold air and the smell of wet wool blew into the room.

"Dude, no way you're ready for that." Jimmy brushed snow off his beanie. "Let me take a leak, then I'll spot you. "

Evan concentrated on his breathing. Before Jimmy came to Astral Projections, everything made sense. Now nothing did.

The day after he talked to Jimmy, he asked Susan to the Christmas concert. She laughed and said, "Thanks, but that's not my thing."

Then, when Bill learned Jimmy went to York without her, he invited Susan to go skiing with him in Vail. After ten days they returned, married. A week later, they took off for their honeymoon in Cancun, and Bill left Jimmy in charge.

Evan boiled with rage. Screw Jimmy. When he walks in here, he'll see me press two hundred twenty pounds like it's a baby rattle. He gripped the bar, exhaled, and raised it off the catch. He held it up no problem, but when he brought the bar down, his muscles cramped. His ears rang. He shut his eyes. Exhale up, he chanted. The bar inched down. His palms burned. With everything Evan had — his heart, his soul — he pushed. The bar slipped against his chest and blocked his air.

WHEN EVAN OPENED HIS EYES, Jimmy loomed over him.

"You are so stupid, Dude. You almost killed yourself."

Evan rolled off the bench and refused Jimmy's outstretched hand.

"I'm fine. Just need a minute to recover."

Evan took small quick breaths and grabbed the pull-up bar to steady himself.

"You so do not get it," Jimmy said. "Come on, I'll drive you home."

"Fine." Evan pulled on his sweatshirt and followed Jimmy outside.

He wished Jimmy never came to Astral Projections, but tomorrow, Jimmy would be in the office showing off his muscles, laughing with the girls, and making money. Evan would be there, too, listening. Later, they would come to the gym and work out.

Somehow, in this time and place, in this astral plane, their lives had come to overlap. They were locked in it now.

Dudes. Bros.

9

POGO'S BRIDGE

1989

From the narrow mudroom window, Willie watched his mother plucking tomatoes from wobbly plants in the small backyard. The window fan spun stale humid air through the tiny row house kitchen. When his mom started for the house, Willie swaggered — Pogo said he didn't waddle, he swaggered — to the refrigerator, opened it, and reached for the pitcher of red Kool-Aid. His mom set three fist-sized tomatoes smelling of earth on the counter.

"Stop! That's heavy. I'll get it."

After she set the pitcher on the kitchen table, she wiped sweat off her forehead and left a dark smudge over her left eye. She wiped her hands in her apron, studied her fingernails, and scrubbed her hands in the sink. Willie climbed the tall chair his father built specially for him.

"I can do things myself," Willie said.

"Maybe you should. After breakfast, pick up your clothes, bring down your sheets, then practice piano for half an hour. By the time I finish hanging the laundry, I expect to hear *Ode to Joy*."

Willie's thick wrists hurt today, and he dreaded the thought of playing piano. Two years ago, the doctor told his parents piano lessons would be good therapy for his gnarled, splayed fingers, but he considered it torture, punishment for being a dwarf.

His mother poured a glass of Kool-Aid, and poured Cheerios and milk in a bowl. When she turned to the sink, he stuck out his tongue. He pulled the bowl to the table edge, clutched the spoon with his stubby fingers, and slurped.

By the time his older brother, Pogo, stomped downstairs and into the kitchen, their mom was outside hanging laundry.

Pogo, who smelled like burned cork, rubbed Willie's head, and said, "Don't drink all the Kool-Aid."

Pogo's boxers showed above his cutoff khakis, and his striped T-shirt was ripped in the armpit. Pogo lined up six slices of bread on the table, covered three with peanut butter, three with globs of grape jelly, and slapped them together. He stepped to the back kitchen and returned with their dad's army kit bag and the thermos to Willie's astronaut lunch box.

"Where you going, Pogo?"

"George and I are riding bikes to the railroad bridge. Then we're swimming in the creek." Pogo sniffed the thermos and wrinkled his nose. "Gross."

After he rinsed the thermos, he poured in Kool-Aid and screwed the lid tight. Willie climbed off his chair backwards, and dropped his bowl in the sink with a clatter.

"Let me come."

"It's too far, Willie," Pogo said. "We'll be gone all day."

At fifteen, Pogo was six years older than Willie. His warm brown eyes turned down at the sides, and his hair flopped over his forehead. He took the bag of Oreos from the top shelf, gave one to Willie, and stuffed the rest in the kit bag.

For as long as Willie remembered, Pogo was his lifeline. No one made fun of him when Pogo was around. When Willie was little — and for him little was REAL little — Pogo carried him in a backpack, making sure Willie could see over his shoulders. Later, Pogo took him swimming in the baby pool at the Y. When Willie's butt got too big for little kid clothes, Pogo went along when their mom took them shopping. 'You can't dress the kid like a fruitcake,' he told Mom.

Mornings, before high school, Pogo walked Willie to grade school and picked him up afterwards. If the weather was nice, they went to the playground, where neighborhood kids played wiffle ball and pickup basketball. If anyone messed with Willie, Pogo went after them, and they never did again.

Willie's bow-legged, sway-backed walk made him so damned slow. Still, when the guys called for Willie to chase down wayward balls and throw them back, they never made him feel like a clown, the way kids did who didn't know him. Whenever Willie told Pogo about a wisecrack someone made, he said, 'Those guys are creeps,' or 'It sucks you're a dwarf, but who cares? That's why they make stilts.' Pogo didn't let him feel sorry for himself.

"Come on, Pogo. Mom wants me to clean my room and play piano, but it's summer. We're supposed to have fun."

It was as hot inside as out, and Willie was crazy to get away. His mom always worried about him.

Pogo tipped his head and stared, then called to the backyard, "Mom, I'm taking Willie on a bike ride to the creek. He promises to practice piano an hour when we get back."

They were three houses away before their mom appeared on the front porch yelling something unintelligible. Willie waved from his seat in the handlebar basket on Pogo's black Roadmaster bike.

The bike wobbled to a stop at George Fitzmaurice's house. After Pogo shouted, "Georgie!" George came around the side of his house pushing his sister's purple Schwinn.

"Fruitcakes ride girl bikes," Willie said.

"Midgets ride in baskets," George said. His large front teeth protruded, and his freckled face shone red from exertion.

The boys rode on the sidewalk, taking Mount Airy Avenue west to Emlen, then Emlen into Fairmount Park. Willie swayed side to side, knees to chest and hands clutching the basket sides.

When they rode onto the bridle path alongside the Wissahickon Creek, Pogo hit a small rock, and front wheel wobbled.

"Yo, Pogo, watch the road," Willie yelled.

"Yo, dorks, watch my dust," George called over his shoulder. He bumped down the path, arms and legs fleshy and white, then skidded to a stop.

When they reached George, Pogo hopped off and pushed the bike, with Willie crammed in the basket.

"This stinks, Pogo," George said. "We could ride if you didn't bring your little brother."

"Remember, Willie, it's better to be short than stupid," Pogo said.

AFTER THEY CROSSED through the red covered bridge, they stopped to eat lunch on the flat granite boulder that jutted into the creek. The peanut butter and jelly sandwiches were squished but tasted perfect washed down with Kool-Aid. They threw the crusts in the creek and laughed at ducks battling each other for the sinking scraps.

From their seat on the boulder, the arched stone railroad bridge, glittery with mica, framed the sky. Willie felt the train before he heard it, a vibration through his spine, then a far-off chugging sound, and finally a high-pitched wail. The train appeared as a dirty silver streak above the bridge wall. It veered left and disappeared on its way downtown. Yellow-tinged dust floated in its wake.

The boys slid off the boulder and walked their bikes to the bridge abutment. Willie lagged behind, moving his short, bowed legs as fast as he could. When the other boys reached the bridge, Willie had to run to catch up.

"You run like you have a load in your pants," George said.

Pogo punched George's arm.

Willie went under the bridge and leaned against the abutment, catching his breath. Sweat poured down his face and soaked his T-shirt. He pulled off his worn Chuck Taylors and dirty socks. His thick feet smelled like burning rubber. He scooted down to the creek and let water run over his legs.

Pogo leaned his bike against the bridge foundation, squatted next to Willie, and flicked water on Willie's face.

"George dared me to cross the bridge," Pogo said, "but it's too dangerous for you. Anyway, we need you to guard the bikes."

Pogo ran his fingers through his sweaty hair and wiped them on his T-shirt, leaving dull finger streaks on the front. He smelled like the creek — damp, earthy, and sour. Willie inhaled his scent.

"I can come with you. I can make it," Willie got to his hands and knees and took Pogo's hand to stand up.

George called from the bridge entrance, "Hey, Pogo, we gotta go now. Your little brother's fine. Don't go swimming until we get back, Willie."

"Stay here and watch the bikes, Little Man. I gotta catch Georgie Porgie Pudding and Pie," Pogo said, bouncing from foot to foot.

"Go on," Willie said, then whispered to himself, "I'll catch up."

Willie dusted his feet, pulled on his sneakers, and crossed the pebbly bank to the bikes. He fished the thermos from the army bag. Kool-Aid sloshed inside, but he couldn't twist off the top. He dropped it on the yellow dirt and kicked it. The sweet cherry smell pissed him off.

George's high-pitched "Last one over gets ten punches," echoed from the top of the arch.

"I'm coming," Willie shouted and made his way to the entrance.

He forced his feet up the rise. When he reached the tracks, his knees and back ached like the time Pogo took him on the Tilt-O-Whirl and he bounced all over.

At the other end of the bridge, George's red head bobbed then disappeared. Pogo was a few steps behind George. As if he heard Willie's footsteps, Pogo turned. Willie waved both hands high to show him he was there. Pogo waved, and followed George off the bridge.

Willie walked about twenty feet to the safety space for bridge workers. Sweat trickled down his face, and he thought he might faint — a head rush Pogo called it. He leaned his forehead against the rough stone and ran his fingers along the mortar between the stones, tracing the pattern Italian masons created a hundred years ago.

Overhead, sun glinted off feathers of a huge circling black bird. Willie stepped on the gravel along the tracks, shaded his eyes, and considered the distance to the other end. He let out a breath. His hips, knees, and feet ached. Pogo was right, it was too far to cross the bridge, and too dangerous. His courage failed, and his body failed. Cleaning his room and practicing piano didn't seem so bad. He swaggered side to side back to the bridge entrance.

When he stepped on the slope away from the bridge, he slipped on gravel and skinned his elbow. Mom will have a fit, he thought, as he wiped the blood on his shorts, leaving a splotchy stain. A dank, fishy smell rose from the creek, so he waited for the guys under a tree.

Sunlight filtered through the leaves and danced on the ground. Willie leaned against the trunk, shut his eyes, and drifted to sleep. A high-pitched whistle seemed far away. He shook his head to wake up and smiled, anticipating friendly waves from the engineer and passengers on the city-bound train. He never thought Pogo would cross the bridge to find him. He never thought that at all.

The train's roar vibrated through his body and drowned out all other sound. Willie opened his mouth in a wordless trill to the tune of the wheels. The engine hauled seven cars, with the siren blasting the entire length of the bridge. After the train vanished around the curve, there was silence, except for birds chirping and water rushing.

The long train and its ear-splitting wail left Willie's heart racing. He was tired, hungry, and thirsty. Now that the train passed, he wanted Pogo to take him home. The huge bird flew in wide, looping circles, screeching and gliding, wings as shiny as black patent leather. Where was Pogo?

About time, Willie thought, when George leapt from the bridge entrance. He looked like a red-haired ghost with ashen skin. George collapsed on the ground, crying and choking like he couldn't breathe.

"Where's Pogo?"

Willie stared at the bridge, searching for his brother. The bird circled above the arch. A dark streak like spilled paint spread down the bridge stones until it reached bottom, and dripped in the creek. Willie watched in wonder.

"Willie," George sobbed.

And then he knew. He knew in his gut, and he knew in his heart that the dark, spreading stain was the blood of his brother. His brother.

∿

2019

THE TRAIN WHISTLE shriek brought Will to anxious consciousness. God, he hated that sound. Thirty-one years after the high-pitched keening at Pogo's funeral, a train's warning blast still made his heart race and sweat bead on his brow. Will read the clock's digital green numbers — 3:16 a.m. He rolled out of bed to shut the window and shut out the sound, even though the temperature this July night hovered near eighty. He toddled back to his rumpled bed, placed his foot on the step stool, and heaved himself in. He flicked on the TV, hoping for something more interesting than how to flip real estate.

Hours later, he woke up drenched in sweat. The small, whirling fan on his bureau circulated fusty air. He felt a deep sense of unease as he rolled on his side and slid his legs on the stool. Now forty, Will lived his entire life in the old stone row house on Mount Airy Avenue. It would be tough to move away. He and his father managed pretty well after Mom died of breast cancer twenty years ago. They hadn't talked much, but really, what was there to say?

When Will went to LaSalle University to major in elementary education, and later when he got the job at Thomas G. Bell Elementary, his father dropped him off and picked him up on his way to and from the Acme Supermarket, where he was the produce guy. Dad brought home groceries each week, but neither of them ate much. Will had to watch his weight, and his father preferred cigarettes and beer for dinner. The cigarettes caught up with him, and last year he died of lung cancer at 69. Now Will relied on taxis.

Eight months ago, George Fitzmaurice's real estate firm bought a condominium building a few blocks from the elementary school. George reserved a handicap unit for Will and sent designers to interview him, to make certain the condo fit him. Then, so he didn't have to deal with people coming in and out, George's firm bought Will's house.

Next week, Will's condo would be ready. He looked forward to a home with everything sized for a little person, but didn't anticipate the anguish of leaving his and Pogo's childhood home.

"Good hair, nice face, sturdy brow," Will chanted to his reflection as he shaved, parroting compliments from his teaching colleagues — comments Will suspected masked discomfort with a teacher barely as tall as his kindergarten students. He gave a skillful flip to the front of his dark brown hair.

Ever since he agreed to move to the condo, he thought obsessively about that summer day at the bridge. Not even his happiest childhood memories of bobbing through the neighborhood on Pogo's shoulders vanquished the terrible image of Pogo's spilled blood. He never had the heart to go back. But now, before he left their home forever, he needed to return to the bridge in tribute to Pogo.

He brewed a cup of coffee, and stepped out back. Next door, Tildy Keating, their neighbor since before Will's birth, knelt at her pepper plants. She was over eighty, a relic, and a friend to the Brennans all these years. After Pogo died, she took in Will for a few nights so his parents could make funeral arrangements. Tildy gave him chores to keep his mind occupied during those days. While his mom never let him crack eggs, Tildy assigned him to break dozens for the cakes, bread puddings, and bowls of scrambled eggs she fed him and his family. Each time tears streamed down his face, Tildy let him cry. 'You loved your brother. Your tears water his spirit so it takes root inside you and lives forever,' she told him. Evenings, Tildy taught him pinochle, and nights when he lay in the cot unable to sleep, his tears watered Pogo's spirit.

During his mother's last agonizing months, Tildy sent over soups and sweets. Later, she helped Will make funeral arrangements. Again last year, after his father died, Tildy helped without being asked. She was unsettled, Will knew, about his moving away, and worried about getting along with new neighbors. Will, too, was having second thoughts, but he needed a place he could manage on his own. Until his father died, Will didn't realize how much he relied on him.

This evening I'll sit on the porch with Tildy, he decided. I'll suggest we talk to George about a condo for her. We're a team, I'll say. We should stick together. Today, though, his mind was made up. Today he would go to the bridge.

He finished his coffee and ate a container of low-fat yogurt. He never satisfied his hunger, but his joints were overloaded by the mass of his torso compared with the length of his limbs. Body weight was an enemy he fought every day.

After he called Academy Cab, he tightened the Velcro straps on his sneakers. With the Internet, finding clothes and shoes that fit was easy. Little People of America posted lists of specialized retailers, and he bought all his clothes online. His students at Tommy Bell Elementary even admired his shoes — 'Nice kicks, Mr. B.'

His hands trembled as he packed a water bottle, banana, and energy bar in a backpack and slung the strap over his shoulder. He checked his cargo pants to make sure his cell phone was safely tucked in his pocket. The wall clock read 9:25 a.m. Outside, a car horn blasted, wavering like the cry of an injured cow.

Will toddled — swaggered — down the stone steps, and crossed the sidewalk to the waiting cab. He waved away the driver's helping hands, swung his backpack on the floor in the back, and heaved himself in. He couldn't ride a bike to the park like they did that day, but he planned to follow the route Pogo took thirty-one years ago.

"Drop me off at the park entrance," Will said.

"Gonna be a hot one," the cab driver said. "What's a guy like you gonna do down the Wissahickon?"

"A guy like me is going for a walk." Will knit his eyebrows. He shouldn't be so touchy.

"You be gone long? You know when you be back? I'm driving all day. You need a ride home, you call dispatch to send Arthur."

"Not sure how long I'll be, but I'll ask for Arthur when I'm ready. You don't mind the small fare?"

As Will paid for his ride, he realized he liked this driver.

"No problem." Arthur tucked the five-dollar bill in his shirt pocket. "You be careful. Those upper trails get slick from pine needles. Don't you worry. Soon's you call, I'll be back to get you, Mr. Will."

The old black man turned the cab around. King Arthur, Will thought. The man must be in his seventies, elderly but still working. He was relieved to know Arthur would return to drive him home.

Will shook his shoulder to adjust his backpack. He breathed in the earthy smell of decaying vegetation along the beaten path to the gravel towpath. It was a lifetime since he walked along the Wissahickon. It felt surreal. He wiped a wrist across his forehead.

Trees along both sides of the path provided deep shade. Strips of light filtered through the canopy of pine, poplar, hickory, and oak. A policeman on a sturdy bay rode by and nodded. His black boots and white helmet seemed too hot for this July day. The officer's billy club tapped a water bottle jutting from the saddle pouch. Will sneezed at the horsy odor, sour and musky like urine.

He moved to the far right to make room for horse and bicycle riders. As he walked, he reviewed his plan. The red covered bridge crossed the creek up ahead. After he crossed through, he'd rest a few minutes. Then the real effort would begin. The path to the railroad bridge was uphill, he remembered. He took a swig of water.

A stampede of footsteps and laughter approached from behind. Will stepped to the edge of the path to let the group pass. A swarm of middle school kids — six scruffy boys and two baby-faced girls caught up to him and slowed.

A boy in a faded blue shirt pointed at Will. "A little man!"

The kid leaned down so they were eye to eye. Christ, Will thought, he looks like Pogo.

"You're a midget"

The boy wasn't at all like Pogo. Will felt the dark-skinned girl breeze past before he saw her. She shoved the blue-shirt boy.

"Shut up, Justin, you're such a jerk! Don't call people midgets." She held herself rigid with fists clenched.

"What? The guy knows he's a midget. It's not like I called him a fag," the boy said before he laughed and moved away.

As the other kids passed, they stared, then took off running toward the covered bridge. The girl stayed and faced him with sad brown eyes.

"Sorry, mister. He's a jerk. We're not all like that."

"Don't worry about it." Will drank some water, fighting to control his shaking hands. "It's no big deal," he called to the girl's back.

~

WHEN WILL APPROACHED the red covered bridge, he listened to the kids' feet drumming across the wooden deck, and watched as they shot out the other side. Across the creek, the blue-shirt boy stopped. He made sure the brown girl was up the path before he gave Will the finger. His laugh whirled across the creek like a spear.

"Crap," Will muttered as the kids disappeared on the narrow path that led to the railroad bridge.

He tried to ignore the deep pain in his hips and knees, as annoying as pebbles in shoes. A drop of sweat slipped past his right eye, a blinding flash and salty sting. He licked his dry lips.

Will swaggered into the covered bridge, grasping guardrails too high for comfort. Using his arm to take pressure off his legs, he pulled himself forward. His fingers landed on green-grey lichen spotting the wooden railing. Soft as velvet, the lichen left a smudge of pale pigment on his fingertips.

As soon as he emerged on the other side, the sun beamed warm on his face. He checked his watch. Tired already, a mere mile or so into his journey with less than a mile to go. A forty-year-old man, no matter the length of his legs, can walk a couple miles through the park, he told himself. You're a man, not a midget.

On the Wissahickon's bank, the flat-topped boulder jutted into the creek as it had for thousands of years. Will sat on a smaller rock nearby. After he ate the banana, he stared at the boulder and pictured that day — the squished peanut butter and jelly sandwiches, the quacking ducks fighting for crumbs. He finished the energy bar and washed it down with water. Sunlight flickered between the trees, and the air vibrated with buzzing insects.

Distant laughter drifted from deep in the woods. Tears welled in his eyes. Stop, he told himself. They're only kids, stupid kids. They don't have a clue. We didn't have a clue either when we were their age. Will pushed himself up, and continued along the gravelly path.

The arches of the stone railroad bridge glistened on the horizon. Will thought about the millions of people who rode the train to the city and back since the tracks were laid in the nineteenth century. As he drew close, he admired the bridge's beauty, its chiseled stones grey and gleaming despite more than a century of sun, rain, wind, and snow. Mount Airy row houses were built of the same glittery stone.

"I've hated this bridge for over thirty years, Pogo," he said to the sky.

As he covered the last yards up to the bridge entrance, his heart raced. He had to sit down. Tears, tears to nurture Pogo's spirit, spilled down his cheeks. He shivered despite the heat. That day, that terrible day. It was his fault, no matter how many people told him it was an accident.

"I'm sorry, Pogo. I never thought."

Will got to his feet, head pounding and vision cloudy. When he stepped on the bridge, he checked both ways along the tracks. It looked exactly the same. This is why I came, to finish the journey, he told himself. He took a deep breath, but self-loathing paralyzed him — a forty-year-old man consumed by a nine-year-old's fear. He forced himself forward until he reached the refuge spot he stopped at all those years ago.

Again Will touched the stones and ran his finger along the mortar. He stared down the tracks to the other side. So far away then, as far away now — too far. If he'd made it to the other side that day, Pogo wouldn't have come back for him. Pogo wouldn't have died.

"I'm coming, Pogo," he shouted to his brother's ghost.

He walked on until his toe caught in a rut and he pitched to his hands and knees. He crawled then, to the center of the bridge, the apex of the arch.

"Here's where you died, Pogo, coming for me."

He got to his feet. He needed to look over the wall, and peer down to the creek where Pogo's blood spilled. He stretched his arms, stood tiptoe, and strained, but couldn't get a grip. He tried again, but scraped his fingertips until his exhausted arms dropped to his sides.

He stepped on the tracks and stared both ways, measuring the distance, calculating the time a sturdy fifteen-year-old boy needed to make it across the bridge. Goddamned seconds, Pogo.

Will set his hands on a steel rail and visualized it coated with blood. What were your last thoughts, Pogo? Did you know you were going to die? Were you afraid?

A gleam caught his eye. He plucked a small stone from between the tracks, grasping the sparkling granite with his finger and thumb. He rubbed the stone between his hands, letting its coarse surface scratch its signature in his palms. The sky was pale blue. He wished the floating clouds would sink and surround him in a thick mist.

Will dropped the stone in his pocket and started back. Somehow, the return was shorter than his walk to the arch.

After he left the bridge, he sidled down dirt and gravel, struggling to keep balance. On trembling legs, he collapsed alongside bushes and brush, and vomited. When he finally stopped retching, he crawled to an old tree — the same tree he sat under that day — and rested.

He closed his eyes but opened them as a distant train whistle grew loud. Moments later, train wheels click-clacked over the steel rails. As Will watched the sleek silver bullet cross the bridge, he felt no emotion. Trains crossed this bridge hundreds, even thousands of times each year whether or not he was here to watch.

Will raised his face to the sun and relished the warmth on his skin. He fished in his pack for his water bottle, and gulped down all that remained. Revived, he got to his feet, and headed for the covered bridge and home.

Scuffling and shouting clattered from the woods. The blue-shirt boy burst out of the trees. The boy's reckless race veered toward Will. The kid's going to run right into me, he thought. He stumbled back and landed on his bottom. The boy, eyes wide, stopped a few feet away.

"You're the guy," the boy said.

"I'm the guy."

"I didn't mean anything before."

"It doesn't matter."

"You OK?"

"I could use a hand to stand up."

The boy, who smelled like the creek, offered Will his filthy hand. He grasped it, and the boy pulled him to his feet.

"Thanks," Will said. "I'm OK now."

He listened to the kids' footsteps drum across the bridge. Before the dark-skinned girl entered, she stopped and waited for Will to join her.

"He's still a jerk, but he listened to me. He's really sorry."

Will smiled. "Thanks. You better catch your friends."

He swaggered across the bridge, marveling at the kids' energy, the way they moved without thought, with incredible grace.

After he reached the path on the other side, he pulled out his cell phone, and asked the dispatcher to send Arthur in half an hour.

As he walked beneath the canopy of trees, he decided to ask Arthur to stop at a store, where he'd buy strawberry ice cream and vanilla wafers to share with Tildy. Tomorrow, he'd begin to pack up the house. He'd fill boxes for the condo, stuff for Purple Heart, the rest for trash.

Will hated the thought of strangers living in his and Pogo's home, but it was time to have his own place, modern and sleek, sized just right.

The path ahead veered out of the trees and up to the street, where Arthur waited. Will stopped and looked back. He dug the rough stone from his pocket and held up the tiny piece of Pogo's bridge.

Flecks of mica glistened in the sun.

ORIGINALLY PUBLISHED AS DEVLIN, PJ. *"Pogo's Bridge." Kaleidoscope Summer 2010: 56-62. Print.*

10

THE LANTERN

A long time ago, the summer I turned twelve, I met a girl with copper hair and wide green eyes under the red covered bridge over the Wissahickon Creek. Her name was Willow. She was thirteen, but smaller than me.

We flicked flat rocks over the creek, joyous whenever one skipped before sinking. Before long, my stomach rumbled. Willow and I climbed on top of a granite boulder where I shared my ham sandwich. Dapples of sunlight danced on her face. With the song of the creek in our ears, we lay back and warmed ourselves in the sun. Sharp caws drew our eyes to the branch of a poplar and the large black bird perched there.

Horse hooves clopped across the bridge's wood planks, and soon, a man on a gleaming black horse emerged. The rider looked our way and waved before he turned the horse left and rode east on Forbidden Drive. I trembled as the horse and rider disappeared under the canopy of trees. The red covered bridge was the strict boundary for my solitary hikes along the Wissahickon. Beyond it, Forbidden Drive led to a mysterious and mystical world I entered only in dreams.

As if she knew my thoughts, Willow leaned on an elbow, and asked, "Are you afraid of monsters?"

"Yes, aren't you?" I shuddered, and my shoulder blades scraped the rough granite surface.

"I used to be," she said, "before I was introduced."

I rolled on my stomach and rested my chin on my palms, studying her. An orange ladybug with black spots landed on her hand. She waved gently, and the tiny beetle opened its armor and flittered away. The scent of pine and damp earth saturated the air.

"What are you talking about?" I asked.

Willow's Story

UNTIL I TURNED SIX, I lived with Mam, my Irish grandmother, in a row house not far from here. To make ends meet, Mam took in laundry and sewing. While she hemmed skirts for rich women and patched men's collars, she sang the old songs —*The elfin knight stands on yon hill, blowing his horn loud and shrill*, and, *When the moon begins her waning, I sit by the water, where a man born of sunlight loved the fairies' daughter.*

Mam knew lots of Irish ballads, and I played at her feet while she sang. At night, when she tucked me in bed, she told me stories about the little people who live under fairy hills. Mam took good care of me, but I missed my mom and dad. I wanted them to come home for good. They lived in a downtown apartment close to their jobs. One weekend a month, they took the train to Chestnut Hill to visit me and Mam.

Each morning before she sent me outside to play in the little backyard, Mam reminded me, 'You're not to leave the yard, my girl. What would I tell your parents if the fairies steal you away?'

Wood fences on both sides of the yard and a thick hedge across the back hemmed me in, but I didn't care. I had no other place to go. I happily built fairy houses from twigs and grass under an oak tree, and pretended to be a fairy.

Moira from down the street visited most evenings to play Monopoly with Mam. I sat propped up on telephone books at the dining room table while they opened the Monopoly board, chose their tokens, and doled out play money. While Mam and Moira rolled the dice, moved their tokens, and bought their properties, I played with the other tokens, imagining the car, thimble, rocking horse, and lantern belonged to fairy people, who used them in houses I built. They especially needed the lantern to light their houses at night.

On a warm morning near Easter the year I turned five, I sat on my stool in the kitchen, and waited while Mam set out my breakfast. After she crumbled a shredded wheat biscuit into a bowl of milk, I covered it with sugar. Mam picked up the laundry basket and asked if I'd be fine for a wee bit while she hung the sheets on the line. She didn't wait for my answer but bustled through the back kitchen and into the yard.

As soon as the door slammed, I shimmied down and peeked outside. With three clothespins in her mouth, Mam shook out a big white sheet, and pinned one end to the clothesline. I hurried to the dining room cupboard where Mam kept the Monopoly game. I jiggled up the lid, squeezed in my hand, and ran my fingers through the tokens until I recognized the feel of the lantern. I pinched it between my fingers and tucked it in my shoe.

By the time the back door slammed and Mam returned to the kitchen, the tiny lantern was scraping my heel, and cereal milk dripped down my chin. My heart raced when Mam wiped my mouth and hands with a dishrag.

That day, I built the best fairy house ever. I pictured the fairy man holding the lantern when he entered the woods before dawn to cut wood for the fireplace. In the evening, the woman fairy cooked their dinner of acorn soup in the lantern's warm glow.

I was gathering dandelion fluff to make beds, so deep in fairyland that the knocking on Mam's door became the sound of village men felling trees. Mam's voice brought me back to Chestnut Hill.

"Mary Crump brought Donald to play with you, Willow."

Donald was a year older and much bigger than me, and I hated him. As soon as he came in the yard, I stood up and brushed off my knees. I started toward the house. I wanted be inside with Mam so he couldn't pinch me, but he blocked the way. His shirt bottom poked through his pants zipper, and his socks were crumpled and dirty. He had a big molasses cookie in each hand and held one out.

"My mom said to share."

When I reached for mine, he jerked back his hand and bit my cookie, then the other. Crumbs tumbled from his mouth and down his shirt.

"I don't want your old cookie anyway," I said. I knelt under the tree and pretended to play with my fairy house.

"What's that supposed to be?" He moved so close I smelled dirt and onion grass on his knees. His shoe pressed against my ankle.

"None of your business," I said in the snotty way older kids used when they passed on their way to school.

Before I knew it, he stomped on my fairy house, and kicked away my dandelion fluff. He kicked again and the little lantern flew against the tree trunk. I grabbed for the lantern, but Donald pushed me and reached it first.

He held the lantern close to his eyes, and asked, "What's this, a lighthouse or something?"

"It's a lantern, stupid," I said, trying to swat it from his hand.

I had to get it back before Mam found out I took it. Donald held it overhead, just beyond my reach. I jumped for it, but he sang, "You can't get it, you can't get it," and danced in a circle.

I stomped and said, "Give it or I'll tell."

"You want it? Go get it," he said, and threw it over the hedge.

"I'm telling my grandmother, and you'll get in big trouble." I yelled, "Mam, Mam, Donald pushed me down and hurt me."

"Shut up or I'll kill you," he hollered, but he turned and ran out the gate.

I waited for Mam to come to the back door. I wanted her to save me from Donald, but I was afraid she'd punish me for taking the monopoly token.

When she didn't come out, I separated the hedge branches to see where Donald threw the lantern, but it was too scratchy. I almost gave up when I noticed a tiny glint. I knew I wasn't allowed out of the yard, but the lantern was just on the other side of the hedge. Once I got through the hedge, I'd grab the lantern and be back before Mam knew I was gone.

I walked back and forth, looking for an opening, but not even a cat could squeeze through the tight wall of branches. I sat under the tree and cried.

A shiny black bird swooped through the sky, then lit on the hedge where it connected to our neighbor's wooden fence. The bird opened its beak, and shrieked, Caw, caw.

I shouted, "Go away," but it stayed on the hedge, staring from black marble eyes.

I gathered a handful of pebbles, ready to punish the bird for Donald's crime. The bird stepped sideways and chirped, Caw. When I moved closer, fist raised, I saw a small gap below its perch.

I dropped the pebbles and slid through the opening. As I squeezed through, I scraped my arm. Tiny beads of blood oozed from the narrow scratch. But I didn't care. I was all by myself outside Mam's backyard, and my body tingled like I bit through an electric cord. I suddenly realized I could do things myself, even forbidden things.

Another sharp caw told me to hurry. I scanned the ground along the hedge, kicking away leaves and digging through pine needles, but couldn't find the lantern. I searched everywhere, staring at the ground, and tripped on a root. My forehead slammed against a tree trunk. I cried when I felt the lump, but even though my head hurt, I kept looking for the lantern. I had no idea how far Donald threw it, so I searched deeper into the woods.

At the click clack of train wheels and the sound of rushing water, I stared up at a long train chugging across the bridge over the Wissahickon Creek. I didn't know where I was or how I got there.

I turned in a circle to find the way I came, but saw only trees, the bridge, and the creek. I was terrified until I saw a child's footprints in the soft earth along the creek. I wasn't alone. I'd find the child and ask her to bring me to her parents, and they'd take me home to Mam.

I followed the footsteps under the bridge, where they faded away. My legs gave out, and I sat on the narrow bank with my back against the rough bridge stones. I stared at water rippling over rocks, and sobbed.

After I don't know how long, I heard the crunch of footsteps. Mam's voice sounded in my head — 'If the fairies steal you away, what would I tell your parents?'

I tucked into myself, and stole a glance. A small girl glided along the creek bank, feet hidden under a pale green dress. I was so happy to see another child, I forgot my fear.

"I'm lost," I said when she sat beside me.

But as soon as I saw her grown-up face on a little girl's body, I got so mixed up I couldn't utter another word.

"You're not lost, Willow. I found you," she said.

Her voice and bright green eyes were kind. She smelled like butterscotch pudding. I rubbed my eyes and wiped my sleeve across my nose. She dug a lace bordered white hanky from a pocket in her dress, dabbed my eyes, then gave me the hanky. I blew my nose like Mam taught me, and tried to give it back.

"Keep it, my darling," she said, her voice like Mam's and her Irish friends.

"How do you know my name?" I asked, sniffing.

"I knew you before you were born, Willow, for you are my kin," she said.

"Are you a fairy? Did you come to steal me away?" I asked.

She patted my arm. "Willow, the world is filled with fairies, monsters, and spirits great and terrible, but looks are deceiving. The most dangerous monsters look like everyone else, and live among us."

"Like Donald." My five-year-old mind understood.

"People who look different, even scary, are called monsters, fairies, and trolls, but almost always their hearts are pure."

As if she summoned him with those words, an ugly troll dragged one leg along the bank of the Wissahickon, and stopped ten feet away.

"Martin will lead you home," she said.

Home! The word sang in my ears. But joy became dread when I stared at Martin. The crooked monster stood almost as tall as Mam, with one sagging shoulder. Hair like hay spilled over his bulging forehead. His fingers were hairy claws. His tongue hung out the side of his mouth, and he panted like a dog on a hot day. He wore a green shirt and brown overalls, but his furry feet were bare.

"Don't make me go with him," I begged.

"Willow, when you confront monsters, you'll recognize them. Take a good look at Martin, and decide," she said.

When I stared at Martin, he smiled in a lopsided way. I turned to tell the tiny woman that even though he was scary looking, I knew he wasn't a monster. But she was gone.

A growl from deep in Martin's throat sounded like, 'Come.'

I followed his wet wool smell to the path through the woods. Three times I fell behind, and he waited for me to catch up.

Before long, I recognized the hedge that bordered Mam's yard. Martin stopped, and motioned for me to move past him.

"Thank you, Martin," I said, no longer afraid. I touched the back of his hand, and he smiled his lopsided grin.

I paused to watch him lumber away. As soon as he disappeared into the woods, caw, caw, came from overhead. When I looked up for the bird, I tripped over that same root, and smacked my head again.

When I opened my eyes, Mam, and my mom and dad were looking down at me. I was tucked in bed with the tiny lantern clutched in my fist.

WHILE WILLOW TOLD HER STORY, the sun traveled across the sky. A cool breeze ruffled my hair. From a branch high above, a black bird swooped down and flew over the creek. I shimmied off the boulder and planted my feet on the soft, damp earth.

"Did that really happen?" I asked.

Willow followed me off the boulder. Rays from the late day sun sparkled on her hair like fireflies. She dug in her pocket and dropped a tiny lantern in my hand.

Willow headed east on Forbidden Drive, and I headed home in the opposite direction.

The tiny lantern glowed in my fist.

ABOUT THE AUTHOR

PJ grew up on W. Wissahickon Avenue in Flourtown, PA, outside Philadelphia. After graduation from LaSalle University, she attended American University where she earned an MA and PhD in economics. Although they never moved back to Philly, she and her husband, John, consider Philadelphia their home. PJ deferred her dream of writing fiction while she pursued a career with Fairfax County government and raised four children with John. She earned an MFA in Creative Writing from George Mason University where she studied with Susan Shreve, Courtney Brkic, Alan Cheuse, and other outstanding writers.

PJ's award winning novels are *Wissahickon Souls, Becoming Jonika,* and *The Chamber, A Wissahickon Monsters Story.*

Made in United States
North Haven, CT
15 May 2022

19197715R00088